BOOKS BY

REYNOLDS PRICE

A COMMON ROOM: ESSAYS 1954–1987   1987

THE LAWS OF ICE   1986

KATE VAIDEN   1986

PRIVATE CONTENTMENT   1984

MUSTIAN   1983

VITAL PROVISIONS   1982

THE SOURCE OF LIGHT   1981

A PALPABLE GOD   1978

EARLY DARK   1977

THE SURFACE OF EARTH   1975

THINGS THEMSELVES   1972

PERMANENT ERRORS   1970

LOVE AND WORK   1968

A GENEROUS MAN   1966

THE NAMES AND FACES OF HEROES   1963

A LONG AND HAPPY LIFE   1962

A LONG
AND HAPPY
LIFE

REYNOLDS PRICE

A LONG AND HAPPY LIFE

NEW YORK

ATHENEUM

1987

This novel is a work of fiction. Names, characters, places and incidents are either the product of the author's imagination or are used fictitiously. Any resemblance to actual events or persons, living or dead, is entirely coincidental.

ATHENEUM
Macmillan Publishing Company
866 Third Avenue, New York, N. Y. 10022
Collier Macmillan Canada, Inc.

ISBN 0-689-11947-X
Library of Congress catalog card number 61-12790

Designed by Harry Ford

19   18   17   16   15   14   13   12   11   10   9

Printed in the United States of America

ch'io ho veduto tutto il verno prima
il prun mostrarsi rigido e feroce,
poscia portar la rosa in su la cima...

D A N T E , *Paradiso,* XIII

A LONG
AND HAPPY
LIFE

ONE

Just with his body and from inside like a snake, leaning that black motorcycle side to side, cutting in and out of the slow line of cars to get there first, staring due-north through goggles towards Mount Moriah and switching coon tails in everybody's face was Wesley Beavers, and laid against his back like sleep, spraddle-legged on the sheepskin seat behind him was Rosacoke Mustian who was maybe his girl and who had given up looking into the wind and trying to nod at every sad car in the line, and when he even speeded up and passed the truck (lent for the afternoon by Mr. Isaac Alston and driven by Sammy his man, hauling one pine box and one black boy dressed in all he could borrow, set up in a ladder-back chair with flowers banked round him and a foot on the box to steady it)—when he even passed that, Rosacoke said once into his back "Don't" and rested in humiliation, not thinking but with her hands on his hips for dear life and her white blouse blown out behind her like a banner in defeat.

It was because Wesley was a motorcycle man since his discharge (or would be, come Monday) and wouldn't have brought her in a car if fire had fallen in balls on every side. He had intended taking her to the picnic that way, and when Mildred Sutton died having her baby without a husband and Rosacoke felt compelled to go to the funeral first and asked Wesley please to take her, he said he would, but he saw no reason to change to a car for a Negro funeral. Rosacoke had to get there and couldn't walk three miles in dust and couldn't risk him going on ahead so she didn't argue but pulled her skirt up over her knees for all to see and put her hat in the saddlebag and climbed on.

Riding like that she didn't see the land they passed through—nothing new or strange but what she had passed every day of her life almost, except for the very beginning and some summer days when she had left for 4-H camp at White Lake or to stay with Aunt Oma in Newport News or to set with somebody in the hospital, like Papa before he died. But the land was there, waiting.

The road passed a little way from the Mustians' porch, and if you came up their driveway and turned left, you would be at the Afton store and the paving soon, and that took you on to Warrenton where she worked. But they turned right today and the road narrowed as it went till it was only wide enough for one thing going one way—a car or a truck or a mule and wagon—and it being July, whatever passed, even the smallest foot, ground more dirt to dust that rose several times every hour of the day and occasionally—invisibly —at night and lingered awhile and at sunset hung like fog and if there was no breeze, settled back on whatever was there to receive it—Rosacoke and Mama and Rato and Milo walking to church, if it had been a first Sunday and ten years ago before Milo got his driving license—but settling mostly on Negro children aiming home in a slow line, carrying blackberries they had picked to eat (and if you stopped and said, "How much you asking for your berries?" they would be so surprised and shy and forget the price their mother told them to say if anybody stopped, and hand them over, bucket and all, for whatever you wanted to give, and all the dust you raised would be on those berries when you got home). It settled on leaves too—on dogwood and hickory and thin pine and holly and now and then a sycamore and on Mr. Isaac Alston's cherry trees that huddled around the pond he had made for the hot air to pass over, choked and tan till there would come a rain—trees he had set out as switches twelve years ago on his seventieth birthday and poured fish in the water smaller than the eye could see and claimed he would live to sit in that cool cherry shade and pull out the dim descendants of those first minnows. And he might, as the Alstons didn't die under ninety.

What Alstons *had* died were the things they came to, after trees—the recent ones, overflowed from the family graves and laid out on this side of Delight Baptist Church, looking shorter than anybody would have guessed, with people around them that never had family graves to begin with—Rosacoke's Papa (who was her grandfather and who by the time he died had completely forgotten Miss Pauline his wife and asked to be buried beside his mother and then forgot to tell them where his mother was) and Miss Pauline, the size of a dressed rabbit, and Rosacoke's own father who was no Baptist (who wasn't much of anything) and whose grave had sunk into the ground. The graves went towards the church, taking grass with them, and then the white sand began that had been hauled in from a creek bed. The church stood in the sand under two oak trees, wooden and bleached and square as a gun-shell box, daring people not to come. The Mustians went and even Wesley Beavers, with *his* name.

But it wasn't where they were going now so they

passed by, and the graves and Delight Church and the sand and the two long picnic tables turned to the woods that Milo and Rosacoke and Rato had run in as children with Mildred Sutton and any other Negroes she brought along (that had scattered now, to Baltimore mostly). The woods began by the road and went back farther than Rosacoke or even the boys had ever gone, not because they were scared but because they got tired—the woods went on that long, and every leaf of them belonged to Mr. Isaac Alston. Once Rosacoke and Mildred packed them a dinner and said to themselves, "We will walk till we come to an open field where somebody is growing something." So they walked on slowly in a straight line through the cool damp air under trees where sun never came but only this green light the mushrooms grew by. When they had walked an hour, they were breathing in air that nothing but possums and owls had breathed before, and snakes if snakes breathed. Mildred didn't like the idea but Rosacoke kept going, and Mildred came on behind, looking mostly *up*, checking on the sky to still be there and to see what snakes were studying down on them. Then they came to an open field the size of a circus ring where there were no trees but only bitter old briars and broomstraw the color of Milo's beard that was just then arriving. They sat on the edge of that to eat their biscuits and syrup and for Mildred to rest her feet, but Rosacoke thought and decided they couldn't stop here as it wasn't a field where anybody had *meant* to grow anything. (Nothing ate broomstraw but mules and mules only ate it if they thought it was something you valued.) So they stood up to go, and Mildred's mouth fell open and said "Great God A-mighty" because there was one deer behind them in

the trees for quicker than it took to say if it had horns.
But its eyes were black and it had looked at them.
When its last sound had gone, Rosacoke said, "Don't
let's go no farther" and Mildred said "All right." They
were not afraid of any deer, but if those woods offered
things like that, that would take the time to look at
you, when you had only walked an hour, where *would*
they end, and what would be growing in any field they
found on the other side, and who would be tending it
there? So they came out, taking their time, proving
they hadn't given up for fear, and when they got to
the road, Mildred spoke for the first time since calling
on God to see that deer—"Rosacoke, it's time for me
some supper"—and they parted. It was no more time
for supper than it was for snow, but Mildred meant to
get home quick and unload that deer on somebody—
his streak he made through the trees and the sound of
his horn feet in the old leaves and his eyes staring on
through all those biscuits at what they did, and waiting.

If Rosacoke had looked up from Wesley's back at
the woods, she might have remembered that day and
how it was only nine years ago and here she was headed
to bury that same Mildred, and was that black-eyed
deer still waiting, and did *he* belong to Mr. Isaac?—
that deer? But she didn't look up and she didn't
remember. If you were with Wesley Beavers, what good
was remembering? You couldn't tell him what you
remembered. He said he lived in the present, and that
meant that maybe when he went a hundred and thirty
miles from home to spend three years in the U.S. Navy,
lounging around in a tight uniform fixing radios and
not moving a step out of Norfolk, Virginia (or so he
said) except to come home a few weekends, maybe he
seldom thought of her. Not the way she thought of

him anyhow—wondering every night if she was his, hoping she was, even when he didn't write for weeks and then sent sassy post cards. But he had been home a civilian three days now, and tomorrow he was headed back to Norfolk to sell motorcycles with a friend of his, and she didn't know a thing she hadn't known for years—which was that he still came to get her Saturday night and took her to a place called Danceland and danced with every woman there in succession so fast he seemed to be ten Wesleys or a dozen, swarming, and then rode her home and kissed her good night for an hour, without a question or a word.

She thought that through once. It was the deepest thinking she could manage on a motorcycle with dust running up her legs, and she was just changing to something new—that at last Wesley had found the vehicle he was meant for (being with Wesley had always been like being on a motorcycle)—when she felt the shift of his shoulders under her cheek and his hips under her hands. The way he moved she slackened her grip for a second. It was too much like holding your eye through the lid while it turns, smooth in the socket but easy to ruin.

She looked up and they were at Mount Moriah Church where they meant to be, and Wesley was turning in, not slowing up at all but gouging a great rut in the dusty yard. He stuck out a leg and his black ankle boots plowed a little way, and that halted them under the one low tree. The coon tails relaxed but Wesley kept the motor going, racing it with twitches of his hand, listening as if he expected it to speak, till Rosacoke said in his ear, "Hush your noise, Wesley."

"Don't it sound funny to you?"

"No," she said. So he let the motor die, and in the

astonished quiet where every bird had surrendered to Wesley's roar, the only sound was that truck and the cars coming on behind, rumbling like distant buffaloes, with Mildred. "Get down, Wesley. They'll all be here in a minute." Wesley swung off the seat and watched while Rosacoke got herself down. Now they were still, the heat settled back on them, and they both shook their heads under the burden. But they didn't speak. They had given up talking about it long ago. Rosacoke took out her handkerchief and wiped her face before the sweat could streak the dust. She looked in the round mirror on the handlebars and combed out her hair that had the wind in it still after the ride. With the black tree behind her, you could see the dust fly up around her head from out of her hair, and in the round mirror it outlined her with a sudden halo. Even Wesley noticed that. Then she put on her hat and said, "We didn't need to come *that* quick" and took off towards the church, sinking through the thin crust of ground with her high heels. When she had walked ten yards alone and her white shoes were tan, she turned and said, "*Come* on, Wesley. Let's don't be standing around staring when they get here."

"Well, I'm going to work on this motor awhile to make sure we can get out when we want to. I'll be in there in a little bit. You just save me a seat by the window."

She only blushed—all she ever did now when Wesley let her down (which pretty nearly kept her blushing non-stop)—and said, "Don't go playing that harp" (the harmonica was another thing he had taken up in the Navy) and climbed the steps. She stopped at the top and looked back towards the road. That way, Wesley saw her and thought how far she had come in three years to being this—tall almost as he was, maybe five foot-nine, and her skin pale as candles laid close on her long bones, and what wind there was, twitching at her hair pulled to the back of her neck, falling down long and dry and the color of straw from under her level hat, stopping below her shoulders where your hand would have been if you had been holding her and dancing with her, close (the only way Wesley danced since his discharge). Then his eyes moved on. And every time he passed below her swinging hair— looking—he got onto women he knew in Norfolk or at the beach and how they smelled, twisting in the dark, and how their smell stayed on him now he didn't recollect their names or how they looked though he had labored in them whole nights of his life and the feel of them was on his fingers like oil, real as if they were by him now under that tree, calling him Junior with their hands working and him starting and them crying "Sweet Jesus!" to him in the night.

But suddenly a bird sang in the tree over Wesley's head, holding up its one clear voice like a deed in the scorching day, and Rosacoke looked at Wesley as if he might have done it—that song—looking clear through him and all he thought, it seemed, shaking her head at what she saw. But Wesley was twenty-two years old his last birthday, and what was so wrong, he wanted to know, with thinking all those things?—except maybe they didn't fit Rosacoke, not the way she was now, new and changed since the times three years ago when they went in to shows in Warrenton and drove nearly home and stopped and spent an hour or longer telling each other good night with the windows misted up, sitting under a tree with pecans falling on the car to make them laugh. Those other women, he had touched and claimed whenever he needed to, but how much of Rosacoke had he touched? Knowing her all that time, how much of her could he see whenever his eyes were closed? How much of her could he claim?—her standing on church steps in Sunday white, straining to see where Mildred was—how much of that could he just walk up and ask for and get?

He might have tried to find out if she hadn't turned and vanished in the dark church, not meaning to roll her hips but letting loose all the power she had there (which was enough to grind rocks) and showing, last thing, her white ankles flexing firm on her heels, and Jesus, he was back in Norfolk sure as the sun poured down. And it did—all over Wesley Beavers from head to foot which was half the trouble. So to change the subject he took out his cycle tools and tightened screws that were tighter already than God ever meant them to be.

Rosacoke remembered in the vestibule that she hadn't been here since the day she slipped off with Mildred and came to the meeting where Aunt Mannie Mayfield stood at age eighty and named the fathers of all her children, far as she could recall. Rosacoke looked round now and the same three things to notice were there—a bell rope hanging from the steeple for anybody to pull, and a gray paper hornets' nest (built in the window by mistake during the war but deserted now far as the eye could see though nobody would tear it down for fear one hornet might be there still, getting older and meaner), and by the open door to the auditorium, a paper bag nailed to the wall with a note saying, *Kindly Leave Gum Here*. She took one deep breath—as if it was the last she would get all afternoon—and went in, and the hot air came out to meet her like a member.

It looked empty—just a choir at the back around a piano and a pulpit in front of that and on the side a stove and then hard seats enough for a hundred people though it would hold half again that many for anything special like a funeral, but it gave no signs of a funeral today. There was not a flower in sight—they were coming with Mildred in the truck—and nobody had thought to come ahead and open the windows. There were six long windows and Rosacoke picked the back one on the left to open and sit by. She went towards it up the bare aisle, and when she got to the pew, the church wasn't empty at all—there was Landon Allgood laid out asleep, the size of a dry cornstalk, breathing heavy, one arm hanging off the bench to the floor and his shirt buttoned right to the neck. He lived alone in a one-room house a little beyond the church and dug graves for white folks, and his trouble was, he took paregoric when he could get it which was mostly on Saturday and then seldom made it home. You were liable to find him anywhere Sunday morning, asleep. One Christmas before Rosacoke was born, he fell down in the public road, and whoever found him next morning had to carry him to Rocky Mount Hospital and have all his toes cut off that had frozen solid in his shoes. That was why, to this day, his shoes turned up at the ends. Rosacoke didn't know how long he had been there or whether he was ready to leave, but she knew he ought to go before the others came as he wasn't dressed for a funeral so she said "Landon." (She wasn't scared of Landon. She had gone in the store herself and bought him bottles of paregoric with his quarters when she was little and nobody would sell him another drop.) She said "Landon, wake up." But he slept on. "Landon, this is Miss Rosacoke. You get up from there."

He was ready. He opened his eyes and said, "Good morning, Miss Rosacoke" just as if he had met her in the road on the way to work.

"It's afternoon, Landon, and will you please get up and go home?"

"Yes'm," he said, sitting up, noticing he was in church and smiling, "Here I am again." Then "What you doing here, Miss Rosacoke?"

"They are burying Mildred."

"What's wrong with Mildred?"

"She died."

"Well, I do say." He got to his feet and put on his cap and tipped it to her and headed as best he could for the door by the choir that led out back. Rosacoke went on into the pew and raised the window. When Landon got to the door—he even had his hand on the knob—he turned and said, "I'm some kin to Mildred, ain't I?"

"Her uncle I guess."

"Yes'm, that's it." Then he could leave.

The church sat sideways to Wesley's tree and the road, and Rosacoke could stay by her window and see what happened in the yard. Landon wasn't ten feet out the back when the truck turned in, having a little trouble with the ruts Wesley made and bringing twelve cars behind it, each one paler with dust than the one before and all packed full. The cars unloaded in order and the first two women were Mildred's mother Mary and Mildred's sister Estelle who had stayed at home when all the others scattered because of her health which was poor from the night Manson Hargrove shot her at a dance, both barrels in the chest. (She lived though—shooting Estelle's bosom was like shooting a feather bed.) Then came the little boys that belonged to most anybody. They were brought to help carry the flowers, but when they swarmed out and saw Wesley, they took off towards him and stood in a tight dark ring, staring out at his cycle like the Chariot of God that could fly. But Wesley had stopped his tinkering when Mildred arrived. He answered one or two questions the boys asked—"What do it burn?" and he told them "Coal"—and then nodded good afternoon to Mary and shut up and leaned against the tree. Somebody called out, "You boys come get these flowers." They went over and took up the wreaths and brought them towards the church, and the one in front wore roses around his neck like a horse that has won and can smile.

Mary and Estelle stood by the truck, looking, and that boy kept his eyes and his foot flat on the box as if it was his and nobody was getting it. Then the other women came up, silent. One of them—Aunt Mannie Mayfield who had walked four miles to get there and was so old she didn't remember a soul now she *was* there—hugged Mary and said what seemed to be a signal, and they climbed the steps—two girls nearly lifting Aunt Mannie who could walk any distance but *up* and who would be next. But the men stayed by the truck, and when the flowers had gone, that boy leaned over and shoved the box to the end, and Sammy and three others took it (to say they had, any two could have carried it alone). They stood a minute with it on their shoulders, taking their bearings. Somebody laughed high and clear. The preacher turned to the church and all the men followed.

Rosacoke saw that and thought every minute Wesley would break loose and take his seat beside her. But he didn't, not even when the yard was empty, and when she heard Mary and Estelle leading the others in, she had to take her eyes off him and stand and nod to the people as they passed and call them by name—the family taking the front pew and sitting as if something pressed them and the others filling in behind, leaving Rosacoke her empty pew at the back, and all standing up—except the ones with babies—till the box was laid on two sawhorses in front of the pulpit, and a boy laid flowers on the lid over what he reckoned was Mildred's face—one design, the Bleeding Heart that Rosacoke sent at Mary's request (white carnations with roses for blood at the center, which would take some time to pay for). When that was done five women stood in various pews and walked to the choir. The piano started and stopped and for a second there was just Bessie Williams' voice slicing through the heat with six high words, calling the others to follow. It was "Precious Name, Show Me Your Face," and it was Jesus they were singing to—meaning it, looking up at the roof to hornets' nests and spiders as if it might all roll away and show them what they asked to see. But the song ended and Rev. Mingie thanked the ladies and said Mrs. Ransom had composed the obituary and would read it now. Mrs. Ransom stood where she was, smiling, and turned to face Mary and Estelle and read off the paper she held, "Miss Mildred Sutton was born in 1936 in the bed where she died. Her mother is Mary Sutton of this community, and her father was

Wallace Sutton, whereabouts unknown, but who worked some years for the Highway and before that, said he fought in France and got gassed and buried alive and was never the same again. She had a brother and three sisters, and they are living in Baltimore and Philadelphia—except Estelle who is with us here—and are unable to come but have sent telegrams of their grief which will be read later. She grew up all around here and worked in cotton for Mr. Isaac Alston and went to school off and on till she started cooking for the Drakes and tending to their children that she loved like they were hers. She worked for them nearly two years, and they would surely be here today if they were not vacationing up at Willoughby Beach. Mildred aimed to go with them right to the last and then wasn't able. She stayed here and died not far from her twenty-first birthday. Her favorite tune was 'Annie Laurie' which she learned from Miss Rosacoke Mustian who is with us today, representing the white friends, and I will sing it now at her mother's request." And standing where she was, she sang it through alone, not to any tune Rosacoke had ever heard but making it on the air as she went, knowing Mildred would never object to that.

Then the preacher read the telegrams. They were all very much like the one from Alec her brother—"Thinking today of little sister and sorry the car is broke." That seemed sufficient reason. Everybody nodded their heads and one or two said "Amen."

Rosacoke sat through that, trying to see past flapping fans to the box. Every once in awhile somebody would turn to see was she there and, seeing her, smile as though the whole afternoon would fold under if she didn't watch it with her familiar face (the way a boy three rows ahead watched her, holding her in his gaze like some new thing, untried, that might go up in smoke any minute). It was that hot inside and her mind worked slowly back through spring water and shade till she was almost in the night with Wesley, but the voice came at her faintly where she was—"Miss Rosacoke, will you kindly view the body?" It was the preacher standing by her, and she turned from the window—"Now?"

"Yes'm, she is ready." They had uncovered Mildred and they wanted Rosacoke to see her first. Mama had warned her this would happen, but there didn't seem to be a way out. She stood up, hoping the preacher would walk with her (and he did, a few feet behind), and went to the box, setting her eyes on the pulpit behind it so she wouldn't see Mildred the whole way.

They had laid Mildred in a pink nightgown that tied at the throat and had belonged to the lady she cooked for, but she had shrunk to nothing this last week as if her life was so much weight, and the gown was half empty. She never had much bosom—Estelle got most of that and when they were twelve, Rosacoke told her, "Mildred, why don't you buy some stuffing? Your bosoms look like fried eggs"—and the ones she had, swollen uselessly now, were settled on her arms that lay straight down her sides and left her hands out of sight that were her good feature. Sometime during the ride her body had twisted to the left, and her profile crushed bitterly into the pillow. Whoever took off the lid had left her alone. Rosacoke wondered if she should move her back for all to see. She looked at the preacher and nearly asked if that was what he meant her to do. But she thought and turned and walked to her seat down the middle aisle with her eyes to the ground, passing through everybody waiting to look, feeling stronger with her part done and Mildred turned to the wall where nobody would see.

And so was Wesley turned away. He was squatting on the ground, and his shoes were sunk in the dust, but he was polishing every spoke in the wheels of that machine as if he never again intended driving it over anything but velvet rugs. The congregation lined up to view Mildred, and Rosacoke had time to think, "To-morrow he will ride it to Norfolk and take his new job and sell motorcycles for maybe the rest of his life, but he can't leave it alone for one hour and sit by me through this service."

And he polished on with his arms moving slow as if they moved through clear thick oil. At times he would rock back on his heels to study what he had done, and his sides would move above his belt to show he was breathing deep—the only way he gave in to the heat. When he was satisfied he stood and cleaned his hands on a rag and his arms to where his sleeves were rolled. But it was grease he was wiping, not sweat. He was somebody who could shine a whole motorcycle in the month of July and not sweat, and his dark hair (still cut for the Navy, stopping high on his neck) was dry. It didn't seem natural and when he leaned against his tree and stared at the ground, he looked to Rosacoke as cool as one November day six years ago, and she thought about that day, so clear and cool—the first she saw of Wesley. He lived three miles from her, and all her life she heard about the Beavers but never saw one till that day—a Saturday—when she went out in Mr. Isaac's woods to pick up pecans off the ground. It was too early for that though—the leaves were gone but the nuts hung on, waiting for a wind, and there was no wind this day—so she was heading home with mighty little in her bucket, going slow, just calling it a walk now, when she looked ahead, and in one tall tree that the path bent round was a boy, spreading his arms between the branches and bracing his feet like he was the eagle on money. It was a pecan tree and she walked straight up under it and said, "Boy, shake me down some nuts." Not saying a word he gripped the branches tighter and rocked the fork he stood in, and nuts fell on her like hail by the hundred till she yelled out to stop or else her skull would crack. He stopped and she picked up all the pecans she could carry, thinking the whole time he would climb down and help her, but he stayed up there and when she looked at him once or twice, he wasn't even watching her— just braced on his long legs that rose in blue overalls to his low waist and his narrow chest and bare white neck and his hair that was brown and still cut for the summer, high above his ears by somebody at home, and his eyes that stared straight out at sights nobody else in Warren County was seeing unless they were up a pecan tree.

"What are you looking at?" she asked him.

"Smoke."

She looked but the sky looked clear to her. "Don't you want to share out these pecans?"—as if bushels of them weren't lying all around her.

"I don't much like them."

"Well, what are you doing up that tree then?"

"Waiting, I guess."

"Who for?"

"Just waiting."

"Who are you?"

"Wesley"—as if he was the only Wesley ever made.

"Don't you want to know who I am?"

"Who are you?"

"Rosacoke Mustian—how old are you?"

"Going on sixteen."

"That's old enough to get your driving license. My brother Milo and me slept in the same bed till he got his driving license, and then Mama said he would have to move."

He smiled at that and she saw the smile was as close to victory as she was coming that day so she said, "Thank you for shaking the tree" and went on home and didn't see him again for nearly a year, but she thought of him in the evenings long as those nuts lasted—him caring for nothing but the smoke she couldn't see, wondering if there was fire somewhere, waiting.

Through that the line went on past Mildred. Some of them—the young ones mostly—skipped by her fast as they could and took a little look and jerked away, and Jimmy Jenkins fell out in the aisle on his way to sit down because he held his eyes shut till he was past Mildred (to keep from having her to remember). A good many took their time though and were sorry her head had turned, but nobody reached in to set her straight, and when Minnie Foot held her baby up to see and he dropped his pacifier in the box, they considered that pacifier gone for good—except the baby who commenced to moan and would have cried if Minnie hadn't sat down in time and unbuttoned and nursed him off to sleep so deep he didn't hear Sarah Fitts when she saw Mildred and wailed "Sweet Jesus" at the sight, but the name went out to Wesley wherever he was (out the window and facing the church but not seeing it, not studying the funeral), and he looked up quick and smiled—maybe at Rosacoke, maybe at the whole hot church—and still smiling, straddled his cycle in a long high leap like a deer and plunged downward on the starter like that same deer striking the earth and turned loose a roar that tore through the grove and the whole afternoon like dry cloth ripped without warning and Wesley was gone.

Rosacoke saw it that way, that slowly. After her remembering she had turned from the window to watch the last ones pass Mildred and to get ready for the testimonials that would be next, but when Sarah released her "Jesus," Rosacoke looked out to Wesley again to see what he would do about *that*, saying to herself, "That is one something he has got to notice." So she saw it from the beginning—his leap—seeing the deer in him as he started and with him still smiling, something even stronger when he reared on his black boots with the calf of his leg thrusting backwards through his trousers to turn loose the noise. She could see that and not think once what he had done or wonder would he come back. She could even turn and watch Mary and Estelle being led to take their last look and breaking down and taking everybody in the church with them into tears except Rosacoke who had as much right as anybody, knowing Mildred so long. But she didn't cry because suddenly the sound of Wesley's cycle stopped—he had taken it up the road a quarter of a mile beyond the church and now surely he would be circling round and coming back to wait. And sure enough he began again and bore down on the church like an arrow for their hearts till every face turned to Rosacoke, wondering couldn't *she* stop his fuss, but she looked straight ahead, not seeing him when the

noise got louder and loudest of all and fell away quick
as it had come. That little staring boy three rows ahead
slapped his leg and said out loud "Mama, he *gone*."
Wesley had passed her by. He was headed for the
concrete road, she guessed, and the twenty miles to
Mason's Lake and the picnic and everybody there.

"Supposing he is gone for good," she said to herself. "Supposing I never lay eyes on him again," and
that made her wonder what she would have left, what
there would be that she could take out and hold or
pass around and say, "This is what I got from knowing
somebody named Wesley Beavers."

There were these many things—a handful of paper
in a drawer at home that was the letters and postal cards
he had sent her. (He didn't write much and when he
did, it was like getting a court order, so distant and
confusing that you wondered for days what he meant
by some sentence he meant nothing by and wound up
wishing he hadn't written at all or wanting to call him
up, long distance, wherever he was and say, "Wesley, I
would like to read you this one sentence you wrote"
and then read him his own words, "We went to Ocean
View last Saturday and met some folks at a eating
stand, and they asked us why we didn't come on and
go skinny-dipping by moonlight so we did and had a
pretty good time and stayed there till Monday morning early," and afterwards ask him, "Wesley, will you
tell me what sort of folks you would meet at a hotdog
stand, and what is *skinny-dipping* please?" But how
could you just pick up the phone and pay good money
to say that when all he would answer was, "What are
you worried about?") Besides the letters there was one
picture of him—a grinning one in uniform—and a
poem she wrote for a What I Am Seeking in an Ideal

Mate Contest (but never sent in as it got out of hand) and a sailor cap he gave her at her request. (She could have bought it for a dollar at any Army-Navy store. She wore it once when he came home, hoping he would take a few photos of her but of course he didn't, and finally she *gave* him the only likeness he had of her, all but forced it on him as a birthday present— Rosacoke Mustian from the neck up, tinted, and looking less like herself than anybody you could imagine.)

That much, then, but wasn't that much left of everybody she ever knew who was gone for good?— the rusty snuff cans that kept turning up around the yard as signs of her Papa, and even the collars of every dog she ever had, and a 1937 New Jersey license plate that hung on the back porch to this day—the one thing she knew that was left of her own blood father who found it the evening she was born, lost on the highway, and brought it home drunk as a monkey and nailed it up over the waterbucket and said, "Will everybody please recall this is the year my daughter was born"— that one thing and nothing else, not a picture, not a thread, no more than if he had been swept away by the Holy Ghost, bag and baggage, in a pillar of fire instead of drunk and taken at dusk by a pickup truck he never saw but walked straight into as if it was a place to rest.

So would there be more than that of Wesley?— anything besides that first November day and a lot of Saturday nights and this last afternoon with him vanishing in a roar and dust? It came to her—what he had said the night before when he was quiet and she asked him if, when he was in the Navy, he looked much at her picture. "Sometimes," he said. "Why?" she said and he said, "Because I would forget what you looked like" and then laughed. Thinking about it though, she reckoned he meant it, laugh and all. He had known her seven years nearly, and when he went that far from home, sometimes he forgot her face. But what was so bad about that? Rosacoke herself when she went to 4-H camp in the summers (and that was for only eight days) would lie on her cot at night, thinking, and suddenly one of them—Mama or Rato or Milo or Papa—would be walking around in her thoughts with no more face than a cheese has got. She would strain to recollect the features and even try to draw out a face in the air with her finger, but sometimes it wouldn't come till she got back home and looked. Funny how when you could remember every mole on President Roosevelt's face and see Andy Gump clear as if he had ever breathed, still you couldn't call up a face you had spent your whole life with. But it never was Wesley she forgot even when he was no more to her than the farthest Arab on burning sands.

There would be the way he looked. And wouldn't that be with her always?—whoever she would meet, wherever she would go even in her sleep—the sight of his face up a tree amongst pecans or down from the tree six years and turned to what he was this afternoon but holding in him all the time that younger Wesley, unchanged and hard at the core, untouched and maybe untouchable but enough like an unlabeled seed, dry and rattling in her hand, to keep her wondering from now on if he might not have gone on growing—that first Wesley—and learned a way to look at people that didn't make them feel ten thousand miles away and to think about something but the U.S. Navy and motorcycles and to talk to people when they talked to him and say whatever he meant and stand still—supposing he had learned all that before it was too late, wouldn't he have made a lovely sight, and then if someday he had ever had to go, couldn't he have left something suitable behind him such as a child that would bear his funny name but have his face and be half hers and answer when she called?

It was the one thing left of Mildred (once they lidded that box again)—her child that had lived God only knew how, dark and hard in the orange crate they lined with white and laid him in, his back curved inwards and his spidery arms and legs twisting inwards to his navel as if something was winding him up with a key or as if he didn't know he was already born and had killed his mother and that there was nothing to call him but Doctor Sledge as no father came forward to tell what his real name was—hard dry little fellow with nothing to go on but half his mother's blood and maybe her looks and the way she used to talk held inside him in case he lived, waiting.

The preacher was waiting too now they had got Mary and Estelle away from Mildred and set them down again. He had intended to have the testifying next, but he could see Rosacoke was studying something besides the funeral so he went ahead and gave his remarks that were supposed to be the last thing before they shut the box—about all of us being raised from the grave including Mildred, but not a word about that live baby no more than if Mildred had died of sore throat. He watched Rosacoke the whole time to see when she would look round and be ready, but she looked on out the window through every word, even the prayer, and when he came to the end of all he could do, he had to say quietly to the back row, "Miss Rosacoke, we all know Mildred thought a heap of you, and it seem like you thought a heap of her"—a lot of people said "Amen"—"and I wonder is there any testifying you could do for her now?" His voice carried and Rosacoke looked round slow and blank as if he had called her from the edge of sleep. To help her out he went on, "If you can find anything in your heart to say, we would be mighty glad." Everybody was watching her. She nodded her head. She had meant to think out in advance what was best to say, but nothing about this afternoon had gone as she intended. She bit at her upper lip because of the heat and stood up and said, "I hadn't seen much of Mildred lately, but we always observed each other's birthday, her and me, and the other evening I thought to myself, 'It is nearly Mildred's twenty-first birthday' so I walked down to her place after supper, and nobody was there except the turkey. I didn't know till the next afternoon they had carried her away. There I was just wanting to give her a pair of stockings and wish her a long and happy life and she was already gone."

That was what she could find in her heart. She wondered if there ought not to be more, but if there was, it was covered now by other things. She sat down and before anybody could thank her, she thought what seemed to be the truth right then—"Everybody I know is gone." In the stifling air she went as cold all over as a pane of glass and took up her pocketbook and pressed her hat safe on her head and walked straight out of church—not from grief, not shedding a tear—but stopping the funeral dead while everybody watched her out of sight and Mrs. Ransom said "She is overcome" and punched Sammy her son at the end of her row and told him, "Sammy, go see what ails that child."

Sammy went and there was Rosacoke on the middle step, hanging onto her hat as if a storm was due, the sun laying her shadow backwards to the door and her just staring down the road. Not wanting to scare her by speaking, Sammy struck a match on his shoe and lit a cigarette. She looked around—just her dry eyes—and said, "Sammy, aren't you burning up in all that wool?" (He was in dark blue—the one man she had seen all day dressed like he knew what a funeral was.)

"If you needing to go somewhere, Miss Rosacoke, Sammy can take you." He said it as gentle as if it was the hospital she might need.

She hesitated as if she was thinking of a map and was on the verge of saying something distant such as —"Buffalo." "I don't reckon so, Sammy. I may have to go home and I can walk that."

"In this heat?"

"I have played baseball in worse than this and so have you," she said. Then thinking what she had done by walking out on the testifying, she said, "I don't intend to ruin Mildred's funeral any further by taking *you* away. Go on back in and tell Mary I'm sorry I can't stay, but I got to locate Wesley."

"No telling where he, Miss Rosacoke, with that machine between his legs."

"No. But I'll be saying goodbye to you, Sammy."

"Yes'm." And she walked into the yard and towards the road in her high heels that were not meant for standing in, much less walking. Sammy finished his cigarette and saw her vanish at the first turn. He was the age of her oldest brother Milo, and this was the first day he had ever called her *Miss* Rosacoke—nothing else to call her, the way she looked, though they played many games of baseball together before Mr. Isaac hired him—her and Milo and Rato (and Mildred and

Mildred's sister Baby Lou at shortstop). He had driven
the truck today and carried a fourth of the box, and it
was generally guessed he was the one might tell the
world what the rightful name of Mildred's baby was so
he went back to where they had given up waiting.
Bessie Williams was singing "Come Thee Disconsolate"
which by now Rosacoke couldn't hear.

She walked in the middle of the road, looking
down. Wherever the dust was thick there would be the
track of Wesley's cycle printed like a message to her.
Seeing that, she would speed up a little and sad as she
felt, smile and think, "What do I think I am—an
Indian nosing out a deer?" But she would come to
long stretches where the dust had blown away, and
there would be nothing but the baked red ground that
took no more sign of Wesley than if he had flown
every now and then. The smile would fade and she
would walk even faster to get to the next deep dust
till her legs, from the knee down nearly, were streaked
with the red and her shoes were fit for nothing but
burning. She could see that but she said right out to
the trees around her, "I will see him if I have to walk
to Norfolk." That thought clogged through her chest
and mouth till she gasped for every breath she got, and
everything else was choked—Mildred, the heat, her
shoes—leaving nothing but Wesley hanging up in her,
not speaking a word, and her at the worst she had ever
been. She couldn't cry. She couldn't speak. But she
thought, "I have spent six years thinking of Wesley
Beavers day and night, giving him things he didn't
want, writing him letters he barely answered, and now
I am trailing him like a dog and him at Mason's Lake,
I know, cooling off. I will stop walking when I get

home and rest in the swing, and I hope he sells
motorcycles till he drops."

She was coming to Mr. Isaac's woods where the
deer had been so long ago for her and Mildred, and
Wesley's tracks that hadn't showed for awhile showed
again—not straight but twisting over the road from
ditch to ditch. She said, "If that is his idea of fun, I'm
glad I'm walking," and she looked up at the woods
and decided to step in and take their shade till she was
cool again.

Between the road and the woods was a narrow
gully from the last rain. She took off her shoes and held
her hat and jumped it and landed right away in deep
moss that was cool with damp from God-knew-where.
She took a look in both empty directions and decided
to go on barefooted so she struck inwards a little from
the road, and when it was nearly out of sight, she
turned and walked on parallel to the narrow dust she
could see through the trees. She was still in hollering
distance if anybody was to pass that needed hollering
at. Working indoors all summer the way she had, her
feet were tender, and she yielded to them with pouts
and little hunches of her shoulders when a stick cracked
under her or a rock pressed up from the ground, and
the sight of an old blacksnake stopped her dead till he
raised up as if to speak and she beat him to it—"Well,
old brother, which way are *you* headed?" and he went
looping off slow over a log and on deeper in the trees.
That kept her looking at the ground from then on,
but once when she stopped to breathe, there was a red
cardinal staring at her from the same bent tree she and
Mildred had called a horse and ridden a thousand
miles. She couldn't think how a cardinal sang, but any

bird will answer you once, however you sound, so she whistled three notes, and he answered just to show her the right way. She told him "Thank you" and tried it his way, but he had given all he meant to give and sat there and swelled up. "What are you looking so biggity about?" she asked him. "You look like every cardinal *I* ever saw." He headed on too for the heart of the woods—north—and if he wanted, he could make Virginia by dark. She called after him, "You better stay in North Carolina, boy. You are the official bird here." Then she wondered, "Why don't I follow him and see where *he* leaves me?" But what reason was there to take off barefooted after a bird?—unless he was aiming for the spring. The spring would be reason enough. She looked back to the road but the dust lay still. Nobody was going anywhere or coming back so she struck deeper for the spring with that bird singing before her as if his heart would burst.

The only path to the spring was two tracks the width apart of Mr. Isaac's truck wheels, left from the days when nobody but he and a few wild children knew it was there. She followed on, picking her way through glossy poison oak, and when she came to the spring (the bird wasn't there, he was halfway to Virginia), it was only a wet circle in the leaves, choked with whatever had fallen from the trees since Mr. Isaac's last stroke. (It had been his private spring that he kept clean long as he could, not for drinking purposes but to cool his feet.) Rosacoke laid down her shoes and hat and bent over and put her hands in where the leaves were wettest—slowly, hoping there wasn't a lizard around—and lifted them out till there was a basin of brown water the size of the evening sun and cold as winter ever got. Looking in it, trying to see her face, she thought of the evening they found this spring—her and her brothers and maybe five Negroes. They had chased all the way from home, hollering some game back and forth till Milo who was leading stopped and raised up his hand like an Indian brave. They halted in a ragged line behind him, and before they could speak, they saw what he had seen—Mr. Isaac there through the darkening leaves, his trousers rolled high and pure cold water ringing round his little bird ankles and him not noticing the children at all or where the sun had got to but staring ahead, thinking. He looked up once in their direction—maybe he couldn't see—but he never spoke a word, not to say "Go on" or "Come here," and directly they all whirled round and started home, circling him wide, leaving him to whatever it was made him look like that. Afterwards, some scorching days they would come and look at the spring and think how cool it was, but seeing Mr. Isaac that once was all they needed. Not a one of them would have waded in if they had been blazing bright from the waist down. Rosacoke had drunk from it though on the day they saw the deer (she had remembered the deer), checking first to see had Mr. Isaac waded lately, then bending over and touching the water with nothing but her lips. She had told Mildred, "Come on. He ain't been here today and it's run clean," but Mildred said, "I don't care if he ain't been here in a month. I can wait. That ain't mouth water no more."

It would be mouth water now—rising up clean for nobody but Rosacoke. Everybody else had forgotten or was long past needing cool feet and drinks of water. She took her seat in the shade on ground that sun hadn't touched since the trees were bare, and she thought of washing her dusty feet. The broiling day was above her, but her feet were deep in moss, and damp was creeping through her dress. "Let the spring run clean," she thought. "I am cool enough the way I am. It will take time but time is the one thing left of *this* day, and when it is clean I can drink. Maybe some water is all I need."

And maybe while the spring ran clean, she could find the broomstraw field. Surely the deer was there and even if she failed to see him, wouldn't he still see her?—peeping through the cluttered woods with his black eyes, watching every step she took, twitching his tail in fright, and not remembering that other summer day, not connecting this changed tall girl with the other one he had seen, not wondering where the black girl was, not caring, not needing—only water, grass, the moss to lie in and the strength of his four legs to save his life. But wasn't it far to walk? Hadn't it taken them an hour to get there, and even if the deer was to kneel and eat from her hand, who would there be to cry "Great God A-mighty" the way Mildred had?—to show it was the one wonderful thing she ever saw, the one surprise. Her baby was no surprise. Rosacoke had met her in the frozen road last February when they were both working and hadn't met for some time. They agreed on how cold it was and wouldn't they be glad to see summer. That seemed all they had to say till Mildred moved to go, and her old black coat swung open—there was her chest flat under a shrunk-up pink sweater that hugged tight to the hard new belly stuck in her skirt like a coconut shell. Rosacoke asked her, "Mildred, what in the world is that?"

"Nothing but a baby," she said and smiled and shut her coat.

"Whose baby?"

"Well, several have asked me not to say."

"Is it somebody from around here?"

"Bound to be."

"And you haven't tried to throw it?"

"What I want to throw him for, Rosacoke?"

"Won't nobody marry you?"

"Some of them say they studying about it. Ain't no hurry. Just so he come with a name."

"Why on earth did you do it, Mildred?"

"I don't hardly know."

"Well, are you glad?"

"Don't look like *glad* got nothing to do with it. He coming whether I glad or not"—and said goodbye and walked away home. Rosacoke had stood in the road, shivering, to watch her out of sight. She went with her thin wrists held to her sides, not swinging, and her fine hands clenched, and when she was gone round the first bend (not looking back once), she was gone for good. Rosacoke never saw her again—not alive, not her face. Mama had said, "I don't want you going to Mildred's another time till they get a Daddy for that baby. The way she's been messing around, they're going to have trouble finding one, and there's liable to be some cutting before they do." Rosacoke had stayed away, not because of what Mama said but because that one cold afternoon was the end of whatever Mildred she had known before. Now Mildred knew things Rosacoke didn't know, things she had learned just lying still in the dark, taking her child from somebody she couldn't see, and what could you say to that new Mildred, her load growing in her every second without a name, sucking blind at her life till his time came and he tore out and killed her and left himself with nothing on earth but a black mouth to feed and the hot air to howl in?

"And here I have walked out on her burying because of Wesley Beavers and his popping machine," she said and stood up at the sound of his name. It was her first thought of Wesley since seeing that bird and it startled her. She said it again—just the name—to test herself. But the name came easy now, not with so much rising in her chest. This was the way she worked—let Wesley pull one of his tricks or go back to Norfolk from a leave and she would nearly die with grief or anger till she could think of something big enough to take her mind off how he looked, not smiling, not answering when she called. Not everything was big enough, only things that had no connection with Wesley such as people telling sad stories or going to walk where Wesley had never been. Sometimes nothing big enough would come, and then there was nothing to do but hope each night the next day would be better, and usually it would (though she had to keep her eyes off pecan trees and not hear rain frogs beyond the creek at night or harmonica music). She would go on that way and finally be all right and free and bothered by nothing but, sometimes, the thought, "How can I say I love somebody who can leave and not worry me no more than this?"—till he came home again, bringing his face like a chain to loop around her neck.

Now with Mildred on her mind, she was free, and from sitting awhile she was cooler. She looked into the spring. It was working but it wouldn't be clear before night. "I will just rinse off my feet," she thought, "and go home and stir up some Kool-Ade and set in the swing and think of what to do for that baby to make up for how I acted today."

She pulled her dress high above her knees and sat again by the edge of the spring and not being able to see the bottom, stuck in her red feet slowly, saying, "If there's water moccasins down there, they are welcome to *these* feet." But her feet sank into cold mud, and brown clouds wreathed the shank of each white leg. She pulled her dress even higher and showed—to herself, to any passing bird—the tender blue inside her thighs that had barely seen the light all summer. Seemed a pity—even to her—having that firmness and keeping it hid (unless she went to Ocean View and showed it to every sailor on the sand). "Well, you're saving it, honey, till the right time comes," she said, breaking the silence above her where the birds had quieted—she wondered when, not noticing them so long. Then she saw the mess she was making of the spring and thought, "I'd be ashamed if I didn't know it would purify a thousand times before anybody needs it again."

But she was wrong. A dim rustling broke the quiet between her and the road, and gradually it turned to somebody's footsteps bearing down on the cracking sticks towards her. "Everybody I know is picnicking or burying," she thought, "and no stranger is catching me like this." She grabbed up her shoes and ran twenty yards to hide behind a cedar. The steps came on and she peeped out. Whoever it was hadn't appeared but there lay her hat by the spring big as a road sign and no hope of getting it now because it was a man that was coming—his shape moved on through the leaves but not his face, not yet.

It was Wesley who broke into sight, stroking through the branches like a swimmer with his head held down and his ankle boots turning in the soft ground till he was beside the spring and shaking his head to see how muddy it was. Rosacoke strained to see on him some sign of where he had been and why he was here, but all she could tell was that, wherever he had gone, he had combed his hair—a fresh part marched across his head like a chalk line—and that he was almost standing on her hat, and what would he do when he saw it? But he looked down for a long time, working his tongue in his mouth as if the next thing to do was spit in the spring and complete the mess, and Rosacoke's hat might as well have been air.

When he moved it was a step backward to leave, and Rosacoke hoped he would step on her hat—then she could speak—but he missed the hat and turned to the road. She took the last chance and stepped out and said, "Wesley, what do *you* know about this spring?"

He reached with both hands for his black belt as if guns were hanging there for such emergencies and hitched up his trousers—"I know somebody has stirred Hell out of it."

"That was me," she said. "I was just rinsing off my feet when I heard you coming—except I didn't know it was you. I figured you was picnicking by now."

He smiled and took another look at the spring and frowned. She walked towards him, holding her shoes. "I don't stir it up *every* day, Wesley. I don't strike out home in the dust every day either." She bent down for her hat—he never moved his foot an inch. "I was watching you from behind that cedar, wondering when you would notice my hat."

"I didn't know it was yours," he said.

"Good thing it wasn't a rabbit trap or you'd have lost a leg." She set it on her tangled hair. "I'll have my name painted on it real big so you won't fail to know me next time." Then she dried her feet with the palm of her hand and put on her shoes.

"You ready for this picnic?" he said.

She looked to see where the sun had got to. It was well past three o'clock. "I had given up on the picnic, Wesley. Anyhow, by the time we got there everybody would be gone."

"Suits me," he said. "There'll just be that much more water to swim in. But Milo will be there, you know, and your Mama said she would save me some chicken."

"Well, I can't go looking like the Tarbaby. You will have to stop at home and let me change my clothes."

"No need," he said. "Everybody will look like Tarbabies by the time we get there," and he took her hand and started for the road. They were nearly at the cycle, and Rosacoke had stood it long as she could— "You haven't said a word about where you tore off to or what I was doing at the spring."

"I went home to get something I forgot, and you said you was cooling off."

"I don't normally walk a mile on a July day to soak my feet."

"If you will hush up, we can ride twenty miles, and you can soak everything you've got."

"I have soaked sufficient, thank you. I have also changed clothes three times today—going on four—and I wouldn't peel off again to bathe in the River Jordan."

"Well, it's nothing but Mason's Lake we're going to, and you can sit on the bank and watch me execute a few Navy dives."

He was already on the cycle and waiting for her, but there was one more thing to ask. "Wesley, how did you know about Mr. Isaac's spring?"

"Somebody showed it to me a long time ago."

"Who?"

"One of my old girl friends." He laughed as if it wasn't so but it was—and laughed on in Rosacoke's head above the roar while she climbed on and laughed still when she laid against his back like sleep, wondering only who that old girl was till they were halfway to the lake and she changed to remembering Mildred. "They are burying Mildred Sutton now. If I had not forgot, I would be there where my duty lies—not *here* anyhow, hanging onto somebody I don't know, streaking off towards a good time, straddling all the horsepower Wesley Beavers owns."

Milo sighted them first of anybody from where he stood at the top of the tin sliding board, slicking back his hair and detaining behind him a whole line of children while he decided whether he would try it headfirst (and risk rupturing a thing or two) or just his normal way. From the top he could see where the highway bent by the lake, and when Wesley and Rosacoke made the turn and were near enough to notice him, his problem was solved—he flipped belly-down on the wet slide and hollered "Here come Rosa" and waved with one hand and held his nose with the other and shot head to toe out of sight in the muddy lake. A cannon sound rose up behind him. (He was twenty-four years old, and Sissie his wife was as pregnant as women ever got.)

Wesley had seen Milo and stopped by the water.

He laughed again with his goggles turned to the spot where Milo sank and said, "I bet there ain't a scrap of skin left on either side of Milo," but behind the goggles he was skimming the whole lake to see who was floating, even while he helped Rosacoke down. She was looking too. They were looking for the same floater, and Willie Duke Aycock was nowhere in sight.

Milo surfaced and stood up in the shallow end near them, every hair on him (the color of broomstraw) curling downward to the lake like streams. He grabbed his groin and moaned, laughing, "Good thing Sissie is already served. *I'm* finished." Then he rearranged everything inside his trunks and said, "Wesley-son, I don't advise you to try no belly-sliding, else you might deprive Rosa of a lovely future."

Rosacoke said "Milo *behave!*" But she smiled and Baby Sister came out to meet them, trailing a string of little wet girls—mostly Guptons.

"You just missed the baptizing," Baby Sister said. "I have baptized every one of these children today—some of them more than once."

"I'm glad you got them before they passed on," Wesley said, walking already towards the bathhouse, taking off his shirt as he went. "They look like cholera chickens right now." The Guptons just eyed him, not understanding—yellow and nosy and slick as peeled squirrels with hard round stomachs poking through their bathing suits and tan hair roping round their eyes raw and wide from so much dipping.

"You two don't look so good yourselves," Baby Sister said and huffed off towards what was left of the Pepsi-Colas, leaving the Guptons hanging in blistering sun.

Rosacoke called after her "Where is Mama?"

"Nursing Sissie over yonder in the shade."

The shade was behind the bathhouse under a close knot of pines that was all Mr. Mason had left, bulldozing his lake, and the remainder of Delight Church's picnic was mostly spread out there—on Rosacoke's right nearest the water, Mr. Isaac Alston in the black leather chair he went everywhere in (that he had barely left since his last stroke), staring at the swimmers and waiting for Sammy to come back with the truck. His collar was undone and there was that line drawn straight through the middle of him—one side moving and one side still—and beyond him was Rosacoke's Mama on a wool blanket, fanning Milo's Sissie who was leaning back, white as fat meat, on a pine with her eyes shut and her hands folded on her belly, not expecting to live, and a little way out of the trees in a pack of their own, a number of Guptons in chalk blue, all exactly alike, set up in the sand straight from the waist as hinges, shoving gnats off their bony legs and lean as if they had never eaten all they could hold (though they had just eaten half a picnic).

Rosacoke was not swimming and Mama had already seen her so she knew there was nothing to do but head for the shade and on her way, speak greetings to Mr. Isaac. That was her duty, as he had been good to them. But bad as she felt, she couldn't face telling him who she was—whose daughter (he never knew lately until you explained and then seldom showed any thanks for your effort). She lowered her head not to see him and bore to the left and circled towards Mama, dusty as she was and blown (with the feel of wind from the ride still working in the roots of her hair), but Mama called to her from ten yards away,

"How was the funeral?" so she detoured a little to speak to Marise Gupton who was Willie Duke Aycock's sister and had been in grammar school with her but looked a hundred years older from giving Macey Gupton the children Baby Sister had dipped. When she got to Marise, Marise looked up with no more pleasure or recognition than Mr. Isaac would have showed and let her begin the talking. All she could think to say was, "Marise, have you been swimming yet?"

"I ain't swam once since my first baby," she said, and her fourth baby who was her first boy and three months old, named Frederick, cried from a wad of blankets on the ground behind her. (Macey her husband was sleeping beside him. He was Milo's age and he couldn't swim.) Marise frowned up to Rosacoke at the noise, but she reached back and took him and laid him on one shoulder. He was hid in a heavy knit suit and a cap that covered his ears (all blue to match his family), and crying so hard, he looked like a fired cookstove.

Rosacoke said, "Don't you reckon he's *frying,* Marise?"

Marise said "No" and that seemed the end of what they could say as Marise was opening her dress with her left hand. Before she was open completely, Frederick rolled down his head and his jaws commenced working. His wet mouth was seeking her breast through blue cotton cloth. "Just *wait,*" she said, a little harsh—to him, not Rosacoke. But Rosacoke waited too, not speaking, and Frederick found what he needed. Marise didn't talk either but watched her baby—number four—pulling hard at her life. In a little, still sucking with his eyes shut tight, he halfway smiled, and Marise gave him a quick little smile in return—her first of the day. Rosacoke might just as well have been in Egypt (and very nearly felt she was) so she looked on ahead and went towards Mama.

Mama said, "How come you didn't speak to Mr. Isaac?" and before she could answer, "You look like you rode in on a circular saw" and kept on fanning Sissie.

Rosacoke said, "If that's what you call a motor-cycle, I *did*."

Sissie barely opened her eyes and said, "I wish somebody had took me motorcycle riding on a rocky road five months ago, and I wouldn't be this sick to-day."

"What's wrong with Sissie?"

"Not a thing," Mama said, "except she had al-ready eat her Brunswick stew when Milo announced about old Mr. Gupton losing his teeth. But there was no way on earth to have told her any sooner. Mr. Gupton was the last man to stir the stew before they served it up, and he had been carrying his teeth in his shirt pocket to rest his gums. Well, everybody had commenced eating their portion except Mr. Gupton, and Milo noticed him frowning hard and feeling his pockets and looking on the ground all round the pot so Milo went over and asked him was anything wrong, and he said, 'I have mislaid my teeth.' *Mislaid!* There he had been leaning over twenty gallons of delicious stew for a solid hour, and where were his teeth *bound* to be? Well, not in the stew it turned out, but nobody knew that till some time later when one of the children found them, unbroken, over by the woodpile where he had dropped them, picking up wood. But as I say, Sissie had eat hers and collapsed at the false news long before the teeth appeared, and here she's laid ever

since, me fanning her like a fool." Then Mama thought
again of what she had waited all afternoon to hear—
"How was the funeral?"

"Mama, it wasn't a picture show."

"I know that. I just thought somebody might have
shouted."

"Maybe they did. I didn't stay to the end."

"Why not?" But Mama broke off—"Look at
Wesley."

Wesley had run from the bathhouse and taken
the high-dive steps three at a time and up-ended down
through the air like a mistake at first, rowing with his
legs and calling "Milo" as he went (for Milo to laugh),
but then his legs rose back in a pause and his arms
cut down before him till he was a bare white tree (the
air was that clear) long enough for Rosacoke to draw
one breath while he went under slow—not a sound,
not a drop and what began as a joke for Milo's sake
didn't end as a joke.

"He can dive all right," Mama said. "Reckon he
has touched bottom by now," and at that Wesley shot
up, holding a handful of bottom overhead as proof,
the black mud streaming down his arm.

"If he's been on the bottom, he's eat-up with
leeches," Sissie said. "I told Milo if he got a leech on
him, he wasn't coming near *me*."

"Wesley is too speedy for any leech to take hold
of," Mama said.

Rosacoke said "Amen" to that.

"I can't speak for the leeches," Sissie said, "but
Willie Duke Aycock has took hold already." (Willie
Duke had had her eyes on Wesley since the seventh
grade when she grew up overnight several months before anybody else, and there she was paddling out to

him and Milo now, moving into the deepest part with no more swimming ability than a window weight, so low in the water nobody could tell if she had on a stitch of clothes and churning hard to stay on top.)

"She can't keep it up long," Rosacoke said.

"Honey, she's got God's own water wings inside her brassiere," Sissie said. (And Sissie was right. Willie Duke had won a Dairy Queen Contest the summer before, and the public remarks on her victory were embarrassing to all.)

"Well, I don't notice Milo swimming away from her," Rosacoke said, at which Milo and Wesley grabbed Willie Duke and sank without a trace.

People in the lake began circling the spot where the three went down, and Rosacoke stood up where she was, shading her eyes in hopes of a sign. Mama said, "They have been under long enough," and Baby Sister was running for the lifeguard when they appeared at the shallow end, carrying Willie Duke like a sack of meal to dry land and laying her down. Then they charged back and swam the whole lake twice, length and breadth—Milo thrashing like a hay baler—before they raced up to the shade and shook water on everybody's clothes and lit the two cigars Milo had in Sissie's bag.

There was a leech, yellow and slick, sucked to Wesley's leg. Nobody saw it till Sissie yelled. It was the last blow of the day for Sissie. She just folded up like a flower and lay back, swallowing loud. Mama stopped her fanning to look, and Milo of course made the first comment—"That leech is having *him* a picnic now"—and Wesley showed he wasn't too happy by stamping his foot. But Rosacoke sat up on her knees, and the leech, being almost on Wesley's hip, was level with her eyes, about the size of her little finger, holding on with both its ends and pulling hard at Wesley's life. She touched the end that was the mouth and it crouched deeper inward.

Mama said, "Don't pull it off, Rosa, or Wesley will bleed to death."

And Milo said, "If we just leave him alone, he can get enough to last till the next church outing, and Wesley will never miss it."

Wesley said, "Milo, if you are so interested in feeding animals, I'll turn him over to you just as soon as I get him off," and he took the cigar and tried to burn the leech's head, but his hand shook and he burnt his leg. "Rosa, you do it," he said and handed the cigar to her. She blew off the ashes and touched the mouth. It flapped loose and dangled a second before the tail let go, and when it hit the sand, it hunched off, not waiting, in three measuring steps towards the water before Mama got it with her shoe and buried it deep till there was no sign left but Wesley's blood still streaming. Rosacoke gave him a handkerchief to hold on the bite, and he wore it round his leg like a garter.

Then everybody could calm back down, talking a little about nothing till the talking died and Baby Sister wandered back and said she was tired and flopped in the sand and sang the Doxology (her favorite song), and when they felt the low late sun pressing so heavy through the pines, sleep seemed the next natural thing. Milo and Wesley stretched out in their bathing suits—hair and all laid right in the sand—and Rosacoke propped against the other side of Sissie's tree, and they slept off and on (except Mama who could never bat an eye till the sun went down) until Macey Gupton yelled his three girls in, and the yell woke up

Baby Sister who was hungry and said so (who was also twelve years old, with every crumb she ate turning to arms and legs). Mama tried to hush her but she woke up Wesley who was hungry too and who shook Milo's foot and said, "Milo, why don't you ask that question you was talking about in the lake?"

Milo came to and asked it. "Mama, what have you got in the way of something to eat?"

"Enough for us six," she said, "and we'll eat it when the five thousand leave." (She meant the Guptons. She couldn't fill them up.)

But it was already past five. The lake had emptied of everything but one old man (not on the picnic) asleep in his inner tube, rocking with the water while it slowed down and woke him up, and the only clue to this being a pleasure lake was the high dive quivering and the temporary-looking slide, and up in the shade the picnic was drifting away. The signal for leaving was when Mr. Isaac's Sammy came back from the funeral with his blue suit still on and drove the truck right to Mr. Isaac's feet and buttoned his collar and lifted him in and loaded on the chair and nodded his head towards Rosacoke. She nodded back and Sammy drove off, and Milo said, "That is the nigger killed Mildred Sutton."

Rosacoke said, "You can't prove that."

Milo said, "No'm, and your friend Mildred couldn't neither. If you back up into a circular saw, you can't name what tooth cuts you first."

Rosacoke swallowed hard but she didn't answer that. Nobody did. They looked off towards the Guptons for relief. The Guptons were all lying down except Marise, but they swatted gnats to show they were not asleep. What they were really doing was *lingering* to find out the Mustians' plans—every few minutes a head would rise up and peep around in case an invitation was on the way. That got Milo's goat and when Frederick cried again, Milo said loud enough for Marise to hear, "What that baby needs is a bust in the mouth!"

Wesley said, "That's what they all need."

Mama said "Hush!"

And Sissie said, "He's *had* it twice already since noon. Don't make her pull it out again."

So finally with nobody saying a word about free supper, the Guptons had to leave. Macey stood and said "Let's go eat" and waved silly to Milo and led off towards the truck. The others straggled on and when they were loaded in, Baby Sister said "O. K. Mama." Mama looked round. The Gupton truck hadn't moved but she guessed it was safe, and she pulled out the stew and chicken and a whole box of eggs (deviled before breakfast) that nobody but Milo would touch.

The Guptons still didn't move—maybe their engine was flooded—but the Mustians were deep in eating (even Sissie) when Mama looked up and said "Oh Lord." Willie Duke Aycock had appeared from the bathhouse door and was heading their way. (The Guptons of course were riding her home. Her family hadn't come.) She stopped at a little distance and spoke nice to Mama and called Rosacoke's name like an item in a sick list and asked if she could speak to Wesley a minute.

Milo said, "Go get her, son," and Wesley went out to meet her with a silly grin that Willie Duke matched as if it was their secret. And she stood right there facing the whole group and whispered to him with her tiny mouth. Her wet hair was plaited so tight it stretched her eyebrows up in surprise, and her high nose bone came beaking white through the red skin, and she had on the kind of doll-baby dress she would wear to a funeral (if it was hot enough)—the short sleeves puffing high on her strong arms and the hem striking her just above the wrinkled knees.

Rosacoke didn't speak a word. She swallowed once or twice more and then set down her supper, not wanting another bite. All she had eaten hung in her stomach like a fist. Milo said "*Sick* her, Rosa!"

"Shut up," she said and he did.

When Willie Duke stopped whispering and went to the truck and Wesley came grinning back to take up his eating, Rosacoke couldn't look at him, but she frowned to silence Milo who was swelling with curiosity before her eyes. Wesley ate on, not alluding once to Willie Duke's brazen visit, and everybody else was looking at the ground, picking at little roots and straws. Finally Milo had to speak—"How many more you got, Wesley?"

"More what?" Wesley said, knowing very well *what*.

"Women trailing you? I bet they're strung up the road from here to Norfolk right now, waiting for you to pass."

Sissie said, "Milo just wishes he had a few, Wesley," but Wesley didn't say "Yes" or "No." And Rosacoke didn't make a sound. The trouble with Wesley was, he never denied anything.

Milo said, "How do you know I ain't got a whole stable full?"

"Well, if you have, Sissie's got the key to the stable now, big boy," Sissie said and patted her belly that was the key.

Mama said they all ought to be struck dumb, talking that way around Baby Sister—around *anybody*.

"We are just joking, Mama, and nobody asked you to tune in," Milo said.

"I'm *not* tuned in, thank you, sir. I was thinking about your brother and how he would have enjoyed this day." It was the first thought of Rato anybody had had for several weeks and they paused for it.

Milo said, "He's happy as a baby right where he is and getting all he can eat." (Rato had been in the Army four months, as a messenger boy. He had got tired of working for Milo—taking his orders in the field—so early in April he hitched down to Raleigh and found the place and said he had come to join. They asked him what branch did he want to be in and he said *"Calvary."* They said there hadn't been any cavalry for ten years and how about the Infantry? He asked if that was a walking-soldier, and they said "Yes" but if he didn't mind carrying messages, he could so he said "All right.")

"I wasn't worried about him eating," Mama said. "I was just regretting he missed the funeral—off there in Oklahoma carrying messages on a Sunday hot as this. Rato knew Mildred good as you all did, and I reckon her funeral was big as any he will ever get the chance to see."

"Why didn't *you* go then and write him a description?" Rosacoke said, seeing only that Mama was hoping to hear about the funeral now, not seeing that Mama was thinking of Rato too.

"Because my duty was with my own."

"Deviling eggs for Milo to choke over? Is that what you call your own? And fanning the flies off Sissie Abbott's belly? And keeping Baby Sister out of deep water? I'm glad you are sure of what's yours and what ain't." That came out of Rosacoke in a high, breaking voice she seldom used—that always scared her when it came. The skin of her face stretched back towards her ears and all the color left. And Milo winked at Wesley.

Mama said the natural thing. "I don't know what you are acting so grand about. You said yourself you didn't stay to the end."

"No, I did not and do you want to know why? Because Wesley wouldn't sit with me but stayed outside polishing his machine and in the midst of everything, cranked up and went for a ride. I thought he had left me for good and I ran out."

Milo said, "Rosa, you can't get upset everytime Wesley leaves for a minute. All us tomcats got to make our rounds."

Wesley smiled a little but Rosacoke said, "Milo, you have turned out to be one of the sorriest people I know."

"Thank you, ma'm. What about your friend Wesley here?"

"I don't know about my friend Wesley. I don't know what he is planning from one minute to the next. I don't even know my place in that line of women you say is strung from here to Norfolk."

Milo turned to Wesley—Wesley was lying on his back looking at the tree—"Wesley, what is Rosacoke's place in your string of ladies? As I am her oldest brother, I have the right to ask." Wesley lay on as if he hadn't heard. Then he rolled over suddenly, flinging sand from the back of his head, and looked hard at Rosacoke's chest, not smiling but as if there was a number on her somewhere that would tell her place in line.

It took him awhile, looking at all of her except her eyes, and when he opened his mouth to speak, Rosacoke jumped up and ran for the lake in her bare feet.

Mama said, "What have you done to her, Wesley?"

"Not a thing, Mrs. Mustian. I ain't said a word. She's been acting funny all day."

"It's her battery," Milo said. "Her battery needs charging. You know how to charge up an old battery, don't you, Wesley?"

Mama ignored him and said, "That child has had a sadder day than any of you know."

"Sad over what?" Milo said.

"That funeral."

Sissie said she hadn't noticed *Mama* pouring soothing oil on anybody, and Milo said, "No use being sad about that funeral. I knew Mildred just as long as Rosa, and she didn't get nothing but what she asked for, messing around. Nothing happens to people that they don't ask for."

Mama said, "Well, I am asking you to take me home—that is the sorriest thing you have said all day, and the sun is going down. That child won't but twenty years old and she died suffering." She took the box of supper right out of Milo's lap and shut it and said, "Baby Sister, help me fold up this blanket." There was nothing for Sissie and Milo and Wesley to do but get off the blanket and think of heading home.

Rosacoke had taken her seat on a bench by the bathhouse with her back turned, and Wesley went down that way, not saying if he meant to speak to Rosa—maybe just to change his clothes. When he had gone a little way, Mama called to him, "Wesley, are you going to ease that child?"

"Yes'm," he said. "I'll try."

"Will you bring her home then and not go scaring her with your machine?"

"Yes'm," he said. "I will." And Mama and them left without Milo even putting his trousers on—Sissie carried them over her arm—and whatever last words he wanted to yell at Wesley got stopped by the look in Mama's eye.

All Rosacoke was seeing from the bench was pine trees across the lake on a low hill and two mules eating through clover with short slow steps towards each other. Somewhere on top of the hurting, she thought up a rule. "Give two mules a hill to stand on and time to rest and like as not by dark they will end up side by side, maybe eight inches apart from head to tail, facing different ways." It wasn't always true but thinking it filled the time till Wesley came from the shade and stood behind her and put one thick hand over her eyes and thinking he had come like a panther, asked her who it was.

"You are Wesley," she said, "but that don't tell me why you act the way you do."

"Because I am Wesley," he said and sat beside her, still in his bathing suit.

The sun was behind the pines and the mules now, shining through their trunks and legs to lay the last red light flat on the empty lake. The light would last another hour, but the heat was lifting already, and Rosacoke saw a breeze beginning in the tails of those two mules. "Here comes a breeze," she said and they both watched it. It worked across the lake—too feeble to mark the water—and played out by ruffling the hem of her dress and parting the curled hair of Wesley's legs.

They were the only people left at the lake except Mr. Mason who owned it. He was on guard in the cool-drink stand as hard as if it was noon and the lake was thick with screaming people.

Wesley laid his hand above her knee. "Let's go swimming before it's night."

"What am I going to swim in?—my skin? This dirty dress is all I've got."

"You could rent one over there at the drink stand."

"I wouldn't put on a public bathing suit if I *never* touched water again. Anyway, why are you so anxious about me swimming? I thought you got a bellyful of underwater sports with Willie Duke."

"No I didn't," he said and laughed.

"Didn't what?"

"Didn't get a bellyful."

That made her thigh tighten under his hand, and she looked away to keep from answering. So Wesley stood up and waded out to where the water was deep enough to lie down and then swam backwards to the diving board with his head out just enough to keep his eyes on her. It was his finest stroke and she wasn't seeing a bit of it, but when he twisted round and rose and grabbed the ladder to the board—she saw that, him rising up by the strength of his right hand, not using his feet at all and hitching his red trunks that the water pulled at. (Even the skin below his waist was brown.)

Then he dived one lovely dive after another—not joking now for Milo's sake but serious and careful as if there was a prize to win at sunset—and she watched him (not knowing if that was what he wanted, not being able to help herself). Once she narrowed her eyes to see only him, and once while he rested a minute, she focused on the hill beyond and those two mules that only had a short green space between them now. Then Wesley split down through the green with his red suit, blurred and silent and too quick to catch.

Before he surfaced, somebody spoke to Rosacoke. "Young lady, what kin is that boy to you?" It was Mr. Mason who owned the lake. He had shut up the cool-drink stand and was there by the bench with his felt hat on, hot as it was.

"No kin," Rosacoke said. "I just came with him. We are the left-overs of Delight Church picnic." She looked back to Wesley who was pretending not to notice Mr. Mason. "He has just got out of the Navy—that boy—and looks like he's trying to recall every dive he ever learned."

"Yes ma'm, it do," Mr. Mason said, "but I wish he won't doing it on my time. I mean, I'm a preacher and I got to go home, and the law says he can't be diving when I ain't watching. He can swim a heap better than me I know—I ain't been under since I was baptized—but you all's church has paid me to lifeguard every one of you, and long as he dives, I got to guard. And I didn't charge but nineteen cents a head for all you Delight folks."

Maybe Wesley was hearing every word—he wasn't that far away—but just then he strolled off the end of the board and cut a string of flips in the air as if to show Mr. Mason *one* somebody was getting his nineteen cents' worth. That time he stayed under extra long, and when he came up way over on the mule side, Rosacoke said, "Wesley, Mr. Mason has got to go home." Wesley pinched his nostrils and waved Mr. Mason goodbye.

That seemed to please Mr. Mason. He laughed

and told Rosacoke, "Lady, I'm going to leave him alone and deputize you a lifeguard. He is your personal responsibility from now on." He took off his hat and took out his watch and said, "It is six-thirty and I am preaching in a hour. What must I preach on, lady?"

"Well, if you don't know by now," she said, "I'm glad I haven't got to listen." But she smiled a little.

And he wasn't offended—"What I mean to say is, you give me your favorite text, and that's what I'll preach on."

Rosacoke said, " 'Then Jesus asked him what is thy name and he said Legion.' "

"Yes ma'm," he said, "that is a humdinger" (which wasn't the same as committing himself to use it). Then he said he felt sure they had enjoyed their day and to come back any time it was hot and he left.

So Rosacoke and Wesley were there alone with nothing else breathing even but those two mules and what few birds were hidden on the hill that sang again in the cool and whatever it was that sent up those few bubbles from the deepest bottom of the lake. There was an acre or more of water between them (Wesley was still on the mule side, up to his waist), but they saw each other clear. They had had little separate seeings all day—his sight of her at the church that threw his mind to all those Norfolk women and her seeing him out the window, rubbing his machine or stroking through bushes to the spring or vanishing under the lake with Willie Duke Aycock in his hands—but this was the first time they had both looked, together. Wesley had his own reasons and she had hers and both of them wondered was there a reason to move on now past looking, to something else.

Wesley found a reason first. "Rosa," he called and

the name spread flat on the lake and came to her loud, "have you got anything I can drink?"

"What do you mean?"

"I mean I am thirsty."

"Well, you are standing in several thousand gallons of spring water."

He took that as a joke and lay down and swam straight towards her over the lake that had been brown in the sun but was green with the sun gone down—the water flat green and pieces of bright plant the swimmers stirred up ragged on the surface and Wesley's arms pale green when they cut the water and his whole body for a moment green when he walked up the narrow sand and stood by the bench and looked again. She smiled, not knowing why, and turned away. Her hair had darkened like the water, and turning, it fell across her shoulder in slow water curves down the skin of her white neck to the groove along her back that was damp. He saw that. She said, "The drink stand is closed." He nodded and walked off to the bathhouse, and she figured they were going home now so she walked back to the pine shade and got her shoes that Mama had brushed and left there and went down to the motorcycle and stood. Wesley came out with nothing on but his shirt over his red trunks and no sign of trousers anywhere.

"Who stole your trousers?" she said.

He didn't answer that. He just said "Come here" and waved her to him. There was nothing to do but go, and when she got there he took her hand and started off round the lake away from the motorcycle.

"Aren't we going home?" she said. "I mean, Mr. Mason has shut it up and all—maybe we ought to go."

"Maybe I can find some drinking water up in them trees," he said.

"Wesley, there is plenty of drinking water at every service station between here and home. Why have we got to go tearing through some strange somebody's bushes? I have had a plenty of that already today."

"Hush up, Rosa," he said. She hushed and he held up the barbed wire, and she crawled under onto the hill with the mules. One yellow hair of hers caught in the wire, and Wesley took it and wrapped it round and round his finger.

"Is that mine?" she asked, stroking her head.

"It's mine now."

"Well, you can have it. The sun has bleached me out till I look like a hussy."

"What do you know about a hussy?"

"I know you don't have to go to Norfolk, Virginia to find one."

"What do you mean?"

"You know who I mean."

"If it's Willie Duke Aycock you mean—she will be in Norfolk tomorrow along with them other hussies you mentioned."

That was like a glass of ice water thrown on her, but she held back and only said, "What is she going up there for?"—thinking it was just a shopping trip to buy some of those clothes nobody but Willie Duke wore.

"She's got a job."

"Doing what?"

"Curling hair."

"What does she know about curling hair with that mess *she's* got?"

"I don't know but she's moving up, bag and baggage."

"What was she asking you about then?"

"She wanted to know would I ride her up."

Rosacoke took her hand out of his. "On that motorcycle?"

"Yes."

"Then she is crazier than I thought she was"—they were climbing the hill all this time, looking ahead to where the trees began—"Are you taking her?"

"I don't know yet."

"When will you know?"

"By the time I'm home tonight." He took her hand again to show that was all he was saying about Willie Duke and to lead her into the trees.

They walked through briars and switches of trees and poison oak (and Wesley bare to every danger from the hip down) with their eyes to the ground as if a deep well of water might open at their feet any minute. But when the trees were thick enough to make it dark and when, looking back, she couldn't see the mules, Rosacoke said, "Wesley, you and me both are going to catch poison oak which Milo would never stop laughing at, and you aren't going to find any water before night."

"Maybe it ain't water I'm looking for," he said.

"I don't notice any gold dust lying around—what are you hunting?"

There was an oak tree on Wesley's right that was bare around the roots. He took her there and sat in a little low grass. She clung to his hand but stayed on her feet and said, "Night will come and catch us here, and we will get scratched to pieces stumbling out." But the light that filtered through the trees fell on Wesley's face, and when she studied him again—him looking up at her serious as if he was George Washington and had never smiled—and when he pulled once more on her hand, she sat down with him. A piece of her white dress settled over his brown legs and covered the pouting little mouth where the leech had been, and she asked him something she had wondered all afternoon —"How come you are so brown even under the belt of your bathing suit?"

He folded his suit back to the danger point and said "From skinny-dipping."

"You never told me what that is."

"It's swimming naked."

"Where?"

"Anywhere you can find a private beach and somebody to swim with you."

"Who do you find?"

"People ain't hard to find."

"Women you mean?"

"Ain't you asked your share of questions?" he said and lifted her hair and hid under it long enough to kiss her neck.

She drew back a little, finally sick from all the afternoon, and said, "Wesley, I am sorry and I know it maybe isn't none of my business, but I have sat in Afton on my behind for the best part of three years making up questions I needed to hear you answer, and here you are answering me like I was a doll baby that didn't need nothing but a nipple in her mouth."

He didn't speak and when she turned to him, he was just looking at his feet that were almost gone in the dark. For awhile the only noise was a whippoorwill starting up for the night, but Rosacoke watched Wesley through that silence, thinking if he looked up, she would know all she needed, but he didn't look up and she said something she had practiced over and over for a time like this—"There are some people that look you in the eyes every second they are with you like you were in a building with some windows dark and some windows lit, and they had to look in every window hard to find out where you were. Wesley, I have got more from *hitchhikers* than I have from you—just old men with cardboard suitcases and cold tough wrists showing at the end of their sleeves, flagging down rides in the dust, shy like they didn't have the right to ask you for air to breathe, much less a ride, and I would pass them in a bus maybe, and they would look up and maybe it wasn't me they were looking at, but I'd think it was and I'd get more from them in three seconds than you have given me in three whole years."

He didn't even answer that. He hadn't seen that every question she asked was aimed for the one she couldn't ask, which was did he love her or didn't he, and if he did, what about those women Milo mentioned and he didn't deny, and if he didn't, why had he kept her going this many years and why was he riding her up and down on a brand-new motorcycle and why did he have her under this tree, maybe miles from drinking water and the night coming down?

He didn't answer but when she was quiet he commenced to show her why. For awhile he did what he generally did around her face and lips and her white neck. And she let him go till he took heart and moved to what was underneath, trying for what he had never tried before. Then with her hand she held him back and said, "Is that all you want out of me?"

"That's right much," he said. And if he had let her think a minute and look, he might have won, but he said one more thing. "If you are thinking about Mildred's trouble, you ain't got that to worry about.

You'll be all right. That's why I left the funeral—to go home and get what will make it all right for me and you."

"No, Wesley," she said. Then she said, "It is nearly dark" and stood up and asked him to take her home.

"Rosa," he said, "you know I am going to Norfolk again. You *know* that don't you?"

"I know that," she said. She took a step to leave.

"—And that maybe I'm riding Willie Duke up there?"

"Wesley, you can ride Willie Duke to Africa and back if she's what you're looking for. Just make sure she don't have Mildred's trouble." So Wesley gave up and followed her out of the woods—her leading because she had on shoes and could cut the path—and when they got to the hill, it was almost night. All they could see was the mules outlined against the lake below, resting now and as close as Rosacoke guessed they would be. Wesley saw them and said "Congratulations, mules."

At the bathhouse Rosacoke kept going to the cycle, and Wesley turned in to put on his pants. But there were no lights in there, and Rosacoke could see up at the eaves the glow he made with a match or two before he stamped his foot and came towards the cycle with his pants and boots in his arms. She said, "Do you mean to ride home naked?"

"Hell no," he said, "but I ain't hopping around another minute in yonder where it's dark and snaky." He switched on the headlight and stood in its narrow beam and stepped out of that red suit into his trousers with nothing but a flapping shirt tail to hide him, and Rosacoke turned her face though he didn't ask her to.

Then not stopping once he took her home round

twenty miles of deadly curves hard as he could, and she held him tight to save her life. When they were almost there she squeezed for him to slow down and said to stop on the road and not turn in as Mama might be in bed. He did that much—stopped where she said by a sycamore tree and turned off the noise and raised his goggles and waited for her to do the talking or the moving. She got down and took what was hers in the saddlebags, and seeing the house was all dark but one door light the moths beat on, she asked him to shine his light to the door so she could see her way. He did that too and she walked down the beam a yard or so before she turned and tried to say what needed saying. "Wesley—"

"What?" he said—but from behind the light where she couldn't see.

And what she couldn't see, she wasn't speaking to —"Have a good trip."

"All right," he said and she walked on to the house and at the porch, stood under the light and waved with her hat to show she was safe. For a minute there was no noise but rain frogs singing out behind the creek. Then the cycle roared and the light turned back to the road and he was gone.

Rosacoke wondered would she ever sleep.

W H E N he was gone three weeks and no word came, she sent this letter to him.

August 18

Dear Wesley,

How are the motorcycles? Cool I hope. And how are you? Sleeping better than us I hope. All the ponds around here have dried up and nobody in the house but Baby Sister has shut an eye for three nights now. We are treating each other like razor blades. If there doesn't come a storm soon or a breeze, I will be compelled to take a bus to some cooler spot. Such as Canada. (Is that cool?) My bedroom of course is in the eaves of the house under that black tin roof that soaks up the sun all day and turns it loose at night like this was winter and it was doing me a favor. My bed feels like a steam pressing machine by the time I crawl in. Last night by 1 a.m. I was worn out from rolling around so I went downstairs and stretched out on the floor— under the kitchen table so Milo wouldn't step on me in the dark, going for his drinks of water. The floor wasn't any cooling board but I had managed to snooze off for a good half hour when here comes Sissie tripping down in the pitch black to get her a dish of Jello (which is what she craves). I heard her coming (I reckon they heard her for miles) and knowing how scarey she is and not wanting her to have the baby right there, I stood up to announce my presence but before I could say a word, she had the light on and her head in the ice box, spooning out Jello. Well what could I do then? I figured speaking would be the worst thing so I kept standing there by the stove, big as a road machine but trying to shrink, and Sissie was on

*her second dish before she turned around and saw me.
That was it. She held onto the baby—don't ask me
how. Cherry Jello went everywhere. Mama was there
in a flash and Milo with the gun, thinking there had
been an attack. Sissie calmed down right easy—for her
—but not before it was sunup and the chickens who
had heard the noise were clucking around the back-
porch in case anybody felt like feeding them. So what
point was there in going to bed? None. Mama just
cooked breakfast and we sat there and stared at each
other like enemies. Before we had even washed dishes,
the sun was hot enough to blister paint and I had to
go to Warrenton and spend the day putting through
telephone calls between people who talked about how
hot it was. Guess what a lovely day I had. I would never
have got through it if I hadn't plugged in by mistake
to some Purvis man telling his fancy woman it was
all off and her saying, "That's what you think!"*

*But the heat doesn't bother you, does it? I wonder
why. Low blood, I guess. Have you ever had it tested?
Being in the Navy, you must have.*

*I will stop now as Milo said he would walk with
me to Mary Sutton's to take some clothes for Mildred's
baby—not much I'm afraid, with Sissie laying claim on
everything here. The baby is living. I don't know why
but maybe he does. The baby, I mean. All I have talked
about is me and my foolishness but nobody here has
done a thing except sweat since you left. I say left—
looks like you left three years ago and aren't coming
back.*

*Goodnight Wesley. It has just now thundered in
the west. Maybe it is going to rain.*

*Love to you from,
Rosacoke*

For that, in two weeks' time, he sent her a giant post card of a baby with a sailor hat on in a baby carriage, hugging a strip-naked celluloid doll and sucking on a rubber pacifier. The caption said, *I Am A Sucker For Entertainment*, and Wesley said,

Hello Rosa, I hope you have cooled off a little bit by now. From the heat I mean. Yes we are having it hot here too but it don't keep me from sleeping when I get in the bed. That doesn't happen regular as summer is the big season on motorcycles and when I am not closing a sale I am generally out at Ocean View where I have friends and can take me a relaxing dip. That is where I am writing you this card from. I would write you a letter but I am no author. I know Milo is having a hard time waiting out Sissie's baby. Tell him Wesley said Ocean View is the place for Tired Rabbits.

—And it stopped there. He had crowded it exactly full of his big writing, and there was no room left to sign his name or say "Yours truly" or any other word that gives you away.

Rosacoke waited awhile, wondering if she had the right, and then said,

September 15

Dear Wesley,

It doesn't seem like a fair exchange—me writing letters and you writing cards—but here I am anyhow because it is Sunday and I can't think of anything else to do. I can't think of anything else but you. (You are no author but I am a poet.) Seriously Wesley, there are alot of questions playing on my mind. They have been playing there six years nearly and tonight I feel like asking them.

Wesley, I want to know are we in love? And if we are, how come you to act the way you do—tearing off to Norfolk after a motorcycle job when you could have stayed back here with your own folks, including me? And not even trying to answer me when I write but telling me about relaxing with your friends at Ocean View and not saying who—just leaving me to wonder if it's Willie Duke Aycock you're riding around or some other body I've never seen. Wesley, that is no way to treat even a dog—well it's one way but it don't make the dog too happy.

I think I have held up my end pretty well and I am wondering if it isn't time you took up your share of the load or else told me to lay mine down and get on home to Mama. So I am asking you what do you want me to do? All I am asking you to do is say. What have I ever refused you but that one thing you asked me to do last time you were here—when I was nearly wild with thinking about poor Mildred and the way I ran out on her funeral to hunt you down—and what right did you have to ask for that when you never moved your mouth one time to say "I love you" or make the smallest promise?

I know this isn't no letter for a girl to write but when you have sat in silence six whole years waiting for somebody you love to speak—and you don't know why you love them or even what you want them to say, just so it's soothing—then it comes a time when you have to speak yourself to prove you are there. I just spoke. And I'm right here.

> Goodnight to you Wesley,
> from Rosacoke

His answer to that was,

September 25

Dear Rosa,

    You are getting out of my depth now. We can talk about it when I come home. I hope that will be real soon as the rush season here is petering out.
    I haven't got any news fit to tell.

Good luck until I see you again,
Wesley

So she waited, not writing to Wesley again (not putting thoughts to paper anyhow) and not having word from him—but working her way through six days every week and staying home evenings to watch Milo's Sissie swell tighter and to hear Mama read out Rato's cards from Oklahoma (saying he had visited one more Indian village and had his picture made with another full-dressed Chief) and sitting through church on the first Sunday morning and not telling anybody what she was waiting for. (Nobody asked. Everybody knew.) And along with the motorcycle season, the hot days petered out, and the nights came sooner like threats and struck colder and lasted longer till soon she was rising up for work in half-dark nearly (and stepping to the window in her shimmy for one long look through the yard, thinking some new sight might have sprung up in her sleep to cheer her through the day, but all that was ever there was a little broomstraw and the empty road and dogwood trees that were giving up summer day by day, crouched in the dawn with leaves already black and red like fires that were smothering slow). And the first Saturday evening in November when she was rocking easy in the front-porch swing,

Milo came home and said to her, "Rosacoke, all your cares are ended. Willie Duke Aycock has got a rich boy friend, and she don't know who Wesley Beavers *is*."

Rosacoke kept rocking but she said, "What do you mean?"

"I mean it ain't been an hour since Willie Duke landed unexpected in her Daddy's pasture in a private airplane owned and piloted by a Norfolk fellow who's *compelled* to be in love—nothing but love could make a airplane land in Aycock's pasture!"

Rosacoke laughed. "How long did it take to dream that up?"

"Honest to God, Rosa, it's *so*. I won't a witness but I just seen her Mama at the store buying canned oysters for a big fry, and she said the family ain't calmed down yet, much less the cow. She said when that plane touched ground, every tit on the cow stood out like pot legs and *gave*."

But once Rosacoke believed him she didn't smile the way he hoped. She stood up and said, "I better go set the table" and walked towards the house.

Milo stopped her. "What ails you, Rosa? You got the world's most worried-looking mind. Willie ain't dropped no atom bombs. You ought to be grinning wide."

"How come?"

"Don't this mean Wesley is your private property now?"

"Ask *Wesley* that."

"*You* ask him. Wesley come home in that little airplane too." He beamed to be telling her that at last.

She turned full to the house and said, "Is that the truth?"

"It's what Mrs. Aycock said."

She didn't look at him again. She went in and set the table but didn't sit down to supper, saying she wasn't hungry but meaning she didn't want to hear them laugh at Willie Duke's flight and tell her to dress up quick before Wesley came. She did change clothes —but nothing fancy, nothing but the pale blue dress and the sweater she wore any evening when she had worked all day—and she sat back out in the swing and rocked a little with both heels dug in the white ground to keep her rocking so slow she could always see the road. What light there was came slant and low in the rising cool and touched a power line of new copper wire in separate places, making it seem to float between the poles towards both ends of the road. A dead maple leaf curled down to her lap. She ground it in her hand and wondered where it fell from (the tree she swung in being oak), and a spider lowered to her by one strand of silk, trying again to fill the air with unbroken thread, and beyond the road two crows called out unseen from the white sycamore that was bare already and straight as Wesley's diving. A distant rifle cracked and the crows shut up. "Mighty late to be hunting," she thought and counted to twelve, and one crow signaled to start again. Then the dark came in. A light went on in the house, and there was Mama at the dining-room window, ironing. (She would stand there till bedtime. Then Milo would tell her, "All right, pack up or you'll have the Ku Klux on me for working my Mama so late.") But the road stayed black and nothing came or went, not even lightning bugs. (Every lightning bug was dead. There had been the first real frost the night before.)

And it frosted Saturday night. Rosacoke knew because she didn't sleep but stared out her window every hour or so to the road till finally by the moon she could see frost creeping towards her—gathering first on weeds low down near the road, locking them white till morning and pausing awhile but starting again and pulling on slow up the yard like hands, gripping its way from one patch of grass to the next and (nearer the house, when the grass gave out) from rocks to dead roots to the roof of Milo's car. Then it silvered that and reached for the house, and Rosacoke fell back and slept.

TWO

Bᴜᴛ Sunday was bright again and the frost was dew when she woke up, and the road was full of black children creeping towards Mount Moriah, trying their white breaths on the morning air, and carloads of white folks she knew but couldn't see, bound for Delight. Her clock said half-past ten and the house was quiet. They had gone on and left her. But when she tore downstairs to the kitchen, there was Milo dressed to the neck, eating syrup. "Oh," she said, "I thought I would have to walk this morning."

Milo tested her face to see what he should say. "Mama went on with Baby Sister. She said to let you sleep if that was how you felt."

Rosacoke looked in his shaving mirror over the stove. "I may *look* dead but I'm not."

"Well, Sissie ain't feeling good either. She's laid out upstairs so you can set with her."

"Milo, I'm *going*. Sissie will be all right and if she commences having babies, Delight Church will hear it. Just cool me some coffee and I'll get dressed right now."

So she dressed the best she could on such short notice and took a deep breath, and they headed off in a hurry (but not fast enough to ease her mind). When they flew past Mr. Isaac's, Rosacoke looked up through the thinning pecan grove to the house and—to break the quiet, to calm herself—said the first thing she thought, "Mr. Isaac's truck is still there. Reckon he's too sick for church?"

"Not if he's live," Milo said, and they went on by the pond and skidded the final curve, and there was Delight stood up in the morning sun with little fellows weaving round it in games and little clumps of men on this side near the graves, making clouds as they smoked through the last few minutes of air. From the curve Rosacoke looked towards the men, knowing she was safe and couldn't see a face from so far off, but after they pulled in the yard and every man turned to watch and one little boy screamed "Rosey-Coke!" (which was what boys called her), she couldn't look again. She looked to the graves where her father was sinking steady. But she didn't notice that. She could only see Milo searching with his eyes for anybody special in the crowd. She trembled to think what he might say any moment, and she said in the voice that scared her, "Don't tell me what you see." Then she got out alone and walked on straight to the church past all those men, seeing nothing but white sand under her feet. And nobody called her name. She went in just that fast and took her place four pews from the front on Mama's left.

"Have you eat?" Mama said.

"Yes'm," she said and turned to the pulpit and meant to look ahead for one full hour, but Baby Sister faced the people, and Mama twisted round periodically to watch every soul come in and report it. Rosacoke would nod her head at the news, but she kept looking forward till Mama couldn't stand it any longer and punched her and said "*Hot* dog!" and she had to look —because in marched Willie Duke Aycock, grinning like she wouldn't be *Aycock* long, with her new friend that she set up front for all to see (and all tried except Rosacoke who read up the hymns in advance, but he had a little head, and nothing much was visible but his

Hawaiian shirt with the long open collar laid out on his round shoulders. Mama said, "He must not have counted on church when he packed"). The big surprise though was all the Aycocks strutting on behind. Mama said, "They ain't been to church since the drive-in opened." (A drive-in movie had opened across the field from their front porch, and all summer long on Saturdays they sat in the cool and watched every movement from sundown through the last newsreel, which left them too tired for church—and ashamed to come to the picnic. They didn't hear a sound of course—of the movies—but in no time after the opening, Ida their youngest had learned lip reading and could tell them every word.) By the time they had all settled in round the friend, it was going on eleven, and out the windows were the sounds of men coming unseen to join their folks, grinding cigarettes in sand and scraping their shoes on the concrete steps and having what they hoped was one last cough. When they came in the back and scattered down the rows (bringing cool air with them that raised the flesh on Rosacoke's neck), even Mama didn't turn. But Baby Sister saw them all and didn't speak a name, not even Milo's when he took his place by Mama on the aisle. Rosacoke could feel him turned towards her, but she didn't meet his eyes, thinking, "Whatever he knows I don't want to hear." Then the preacher and the choir ladies came in and sat. Everybody quieted except Mama (who said what everybody thought), "Mr. Isaac ain't here. He must be bad off," and not knowing who was behind her and with no way left to find out, Rosacoke thought, "How will I get through this hour alone with nothing to look at but three white walls and a black pulpit and a preacher and ten choir ladies and the back of Willie Duke Aycock's

neck?—not a flower or a picture in sight and nothing
to think of but Wesley Beavers and whether he is ten
yards away or three whole miles and why he isn't here
by me."

The preacher stood up and called for the hymn,
and while the hymnals were rustling, the side door
opened by the choir, and Mr. Isaac's Sammy walked in
with the black leather chair. He nodded to the people
in general, and they nodded back in relief, and he set
the chair where it belonged by the front of the Amen
Corner, half to the preacher, half to the people. Then
he went out and everybody waited, not standing, till he
came again—Mr. Isaac in his arms like a baby with a
tan suit on and a white shirt pinned at the neck with
gold, holding Sammy's shoulder with his live left arm
(his right arm slack in the sleeve and that leg) and his
face half live and half dead, with a smile set permanent
by two hard strokes on the half that turned to the people when Sammy set him gentle in the chair and knelt
to arrange his little bird legs. Then Sammy stood and
whispered some message in the live ear and sat down
himself on a pew by the chair. And the singing began,
with Baby Sister leading them all to a long "Amen,"
low but sure.

So she had Mr. Isaac to watch through that long
hour—the still half at least to take her mind off whatever people were behind her—and she started by thinking back quick as she could to the way he scared them
when they were children, not by meaning any harm but
by stopping his truck in the road whenever he saw them
and calling out "Come here, girl" (or "boy"—he never
said names). They would creep towards him and stand
back a little from the truck, making arcs on the dust
with their toes till he said, "Whose girl are you?"

(meaning who was their mother), and they would say "Emma Mustian's." He would say "Are you sure?" and when they nodded, hand them horehound candy out the window to eat with the blue lint of his shirt pocket stuck in it and then drive away, not smiling once. But the permanent smile was on him now, tame as something made with needle and thread, that didn't have a place in the ways she remembered him—like the day he stopped in the road and not smiling once asked Milo, "How old are you, boy?" Milo told him "Thirteen" and he said, "If you rub turpentine on your thighs, it'll make hair grow" (Milo tried it and nearly perished with the stinging) or before that even, the day they found his spring—her and Milo and Mildred and the others, coming on him sudden in the woods with his ankles in water and the look on his face showing he wasn't there behind it that made them turn and leave without waiting for candy—and the evening her Daddy was killed and Mr. Isaac came and stood on the porch and handed her Mama fifty dollars, saying, "He is far better off" (which was true) and the day he came to see her Papa in the hospital and Papa, just rambling, said, "How come you never got married?" and Mr. Isaac said "Nobody asked me" and smiled but soon fell back into looking the way that covered his heart like a shield and kept you guessing what he was thinking of—his age? (which was eighty-two now) or his health? or all the money he owned in land and trees which he didn't spend and which, since he never married, would go to Marina his sister who cooked his food but was too old herself to offer him love and care?—the only thing that loved him being Sammy his man who had grown from the lean black boy that drove him on the land in a truck to the man who carried him now in his arms.

She stopped her thinking for the second hymn. (Willie Duke's friend more than did his share of that.) Then she bowed her head for the prayer, but once the preacher was underway, thanking God for everything green but weeds, Marise Gupton's Frederick tuned up to cry from the back of the church. Rosacoke and Mama looked quick to Milo to stop him from mentioning busts in the mouth, but Marise stopped the crying and Milo just smiled and they all bowed again. The prayer went on about doctors and nurses and beds of affliction, and Rosacoke looked to Mr. Isaac. She had to. He was somebody that didn't know Wesley, except by name. His head was up and the dead right eye was open, bearing straight to the opposite wall, but Sammy was bowed like everybody round him. Towards the end of the prayer, Mr. Isaac's live hand flickered on the arm of the chair and tapped Sammy's knee one time. Sammy didn't look up (though the live side faced him) and the hand tapped again. Sammy knew and, still bowed, reached in his pocket and took out two pieces of horehound candy that would keep him happy till the end. Mr. Isaac put one in his mouth and hid the spare in his hand, and Rosacoke looked all round (except behind) to see had anybody else watched that. Everybody was bowed, including Baby Sister who took prayer serious to be so young, and Rosacoke said to herself, "I have seen it alone so maybe the day isn't wasted."

Thinking that kept her fairly calm through collection and the sermon and the final hymn—right to the last few words the preacher spoke. He looked at the people and smiled and said, "We are happy, I know, to welcome old members who are with us today from the great cities where they work, and I know we will all want to greet our visitor who descended last night from the clouds!" Then he spoke a benediction and before it was out of his mouth, Willie Duke shot her friend through the side door like something too delicate to meet. Rosacoke thought, "At least I have got out of speaking to Willie," and Mama said to her, "Come on and speak to Mr. Isaac." (A dozen people were waiting already to shake his hand.)

Rosacoke said, "Mama, don't bother him today" and faced the people that were streaming out. Wesley wasn't there. Those visitors from the clouds were nothing but Willie Duke Aycock and her friend so Rosacoke followed Mama, and they stood their turn to greet Mr. Isaac.

He was still in his chair with Sammy behind him now, and when people spoke he didn't speak back or hold out his live hand that was clenched in his lap but bobbed his chin and let the half-smile do the rest till he saw Rosacoke. She came up in line before Mama and said, "Good morning, Mr. Isaac. I hope you are feeling all right."

He tilted his eyes to her face and studied it, still as before. Then he spoke in the voice that was left. "Whose girl are you?"

She held back a moment and said "Emma Mustian's," not sure that was what he meant, and pointed at Mama behind her. But he looked to his clenched live hand, and it opened enough for them both to see the one piece of candy that had hid there since the prayer, damp and soft. Then he clenched it again and looked back at her. No one had seen it but them—not even Sammy—so he matched, on the live side of his face, that lasting smile. Rosacoke smiled too and thinking he finally knew her, told him goodbye and went on quick out the front before Mama caught her and started commenting, and there of course all but blocking the door stood Willie Duke and her friend.

Willie said, "Rosa, come meet my aviator." Rosacoke looked at him. "Rosacoke Mustian, this is Heywood Betts, my boy friend who flew me down."

Rosacoke shook his hand and said, "How do you do."

He said, "Good morning, I'm fine but scrap metal is my work—flying's just a hobby."

Willie Duke waved at some Gupton girls in the yard—her nieces—and said (not looking at Rosacoke), "I kind of thought Wesley would be here today, not being home in so long."

Rosacoke said "Did you?" and looked round as if she had just noticed his absence.

Heywood Betts said, "Maybe he's laid up after our pasture landing."

"Shoot," Willie Duke said, "nothing don't bother Wesley, does it, Rosa?"

"Not much."

Heywood laughed. "He looked plenty bothered yesterday when you talked me out of landing at Warrenton airport."

Willie Duke said, "Nothing don't bother Wesley. He just didn't have his sweet thing to show off like I do you"—and squeezed Heywood tight.

Rosacoke looked towards the car where her people were waiting and then towards the sun. "Sure is bright," she said. "I better be getting on home. When are you all leaving?"

Willie Duke said, "Me and Heywood's definitely leaving this afternoon. But I ain't sure about Wesley. He's took Monday off so maybe he's leaving and maybe he's not."

"Well, happy landing," Rosacoke said and went to the car for the little trip home. Milo drove it fast as he could, and nobody spoke, not even when they passed Mr. Isaac's stripped cherry trees and his pond again that had shrunk in the sun but was so hard-blue it seemed you could walk on the surface like Jesus and not sink. But when they were home and climbed out slowly, Mama put her arm round Rosacoke's waist and forced their eyes to meet—"Rosa, go rest a little. You don't have to eat." That hit Rosacoke like something filthy across her mouth, and she ran out of Mama's arms to wash her hands for dinner.

And everything went all right for awhile at dinner. There was a lot of laughing about Willie Duke's man. Mama said, *"He's* rich. He didn't give a cent when the plate was passed," and Milo said, "Well, rich or poor, Willie Duke has sure took hold—and in the right place." But Rosacoke almost welcomed that. There were worse things now than Willie Duke Aycock, and it looked as if the family knew her feelings and were honoring them—even Milo—till Sissie finished all she could hold. Sissie had come down to dinner late and hadn't heard the news about church so she blurted out, "I thought you would ask Wesley to dinner, Rosa."

Rosacoke looked at her plate.

Milo said, "Hell-fire, Sissie. How are we going to ask him—by homing pigeon?"

"I'm sorry," Sissie said. "I just thought he would be at church and come home with you all—specially since your mother stayed up half the night cooking this mighty spread."

Mama said slowly, "Sissie, Wesley, as you could tell from his name if you had thought, is not a Baptist."

Milo said, "No, but he put in pretty good attendance long as he was interested in the Baptists he knew."

Mama said, "I hope he was at the Methodists' with his mother. That's where he belonged."

Rosacoke spoke for the first time. "Looks like to me all this isn't any of you all's business."

"Listen, Weeping Willow," Milo said, "if you could see the way you look—pale as ashes right this minute—you'd agree it was time somebody took a hickory stick to Wesley Beavers and made him behave."

"Well, don't let that somebody be you," Rosacoke said. "I can take care of my own business."

"Yes, and you've made a piss-poor job of it, honey. He landed here Saturday evening. You ain't seen him for what?—two months? You still ain't seen him and he's setting on his own front porch, not three miles from this oak table."

"All right," Rosacoke said, "tell me one magic word and I'll have him here, dressed for marriage, in ten seconds flat if that's what you want."

"Magic ain't what you need."

"What is it then? God knows I've tried."

Sissie, not meaning harm, had started it all so she poked Milo and said "Hush up."

But Milo was rolling. "What you need is a little bit of Sissie's method." He turned to Sissie and grinned, and she shoved back her chair and left the room. He called after her, "Sissie, come tell Rosa what your uncle said was the way to get old Milo."

Sissie hollered from the living room, "Milo, I got you *honest* and my uncle didn't tell me nothing."

So Milo sang it himself—

Pull up your petticoat, pull down your drawers,
Give him one look at old Santy Claus.

Mama said, "Milo, leave my table," and Rosacoke ran up the stairs to her room.

Half the room was covered with yellow sun so the first thing she did was pull the shades, and when she had made it dark as she could, she stepped to the middle of the floor and commenced taking off her dress. She checked every button for safety and tested a seam and stepped to the high wardrobe to hang it there in the darkest corner as if she was burying it. She unstrapped her wrist watch and stepped to the mantel and laid it there (but she kept her eyes off the propped-up picture) and kicked off her shoes and, still standing, peeled down her stockings and held them against a shaded window for flaws. Then she fell on her bed and cried over Wesley for the first time in her life. But the tears gave out and the anger, and behind them there was nothing. Plain nothing. She couldn't think. As a girl, when she was sad, she would shut her eyes and cast her mind to the future, thinking what a month from then would be like or when she was old, and she tried that now. But she couldn't. She couldn't think what an *hour* from then might be or the next day (which was Monday and work), much less a month or twenty-five years. She turned on her back and stared at the yellow goat's head stained on the ceiling. Her Papa told her it came from him keeping goats in the attic that peed. But he was joking. Everybody she knew was always joking. So she said it out loud, "What must I do about Wesley Beavers? And that's no joke." It was the second time she had asked the question, and the only answer anyone had offered was Milo's jingle that clattered behind her eyes right now. Milo was the closest kin she had that was grown (Rato being grown from the neck down, only), and he had sung that to her.

To cover his song she listened to the only sound in the house that reached her room—Baby Sister on the porch, putting paper dolls through her favorite story at the top of her voice. There was a daughter-doll who worked and one evening came home to tell her mother she had lice. The mother-doll said, "My own flesh and blood and you have lice!" It was the worst thing Baby Sister knew of. Rosacoke thought she would lean out the window and tell Baby Sister to talk a little quieter please or hum a tune, but her own door opened and Mama walked in, knocking down coat hangers as she came.

Rosacoke raised up and squinted to try and show she had been asleep. "Mama, I have asked everybody to knock before they enter."

"Don't make me mad," Mama said, "before I have spoke a word. I walked up fourteen steps to talk to you."

"What about?"

"I wanted to show you this old picture I found when I was cleaning out Papa's chest." Rosacoke gave her a look that meant couldn't it wait, but Mama raised one shade a little and came and stood by the bed. Rosacoke took the stiff tan photograph. It was two boys in pitiful long low-belted summer clothes on a pier with a wrought-iron rail behind them and, beyond that, water. The oldest boy might have been ten, and he had on white knee-stockings. His hair seemed blond and covered half his forehead like a bowl. His eyes were wide and full of white, and his mouth cut through his face in one perfectly straight line. He didn't frown but he didn't smile. He just held on tight as if he had something grand to give but the camera wasn't getting it— not that day. The boy who held his hand was smaller—

maybe seven—and laughing with his mouth open wide. He had laughed till his face was blurred and the one sure thing about him was an American flag in his right hand and even that was flapping.

Rosacoke said, "Who is it of?"

"The biggest one is your Daddy."

"Well, Lord," she said and turned it over. There was her father's name and "Ocean View, July 1915." "I never saw him so clear before," she said.

Mama still stood up. "I didn't believe there was a likeness of him in the world, and then I come across this. It must have been the time your Papa took them all to water for the day. It was the one trip he ever gave them, and it ended awful because he put a five-dollar bill in his shoe in case of emergency and then walked ten miles up and down the sand. About leaving time, emergencies arose—one was your Daddy wanting a plaster of Paris statue of Mutt and Jeff—and when Papa took off his shoe for the money, it was just little soggy pieces. He had wore it out! He talked about that for thirty years."

Rosacoke kept looking at the picture. "Did you know Daddy then?"

Mama said, "Good as I ever did" and sat on the bed. "I don't mean to say we passed any time together —we was nothing but babies—but I used to see him sometime at church, and at Sunday school picnics he generally wound up eating on us. He never did like Miss Pauline's cooking, and chicken pies was all she brought to picnics." She held out her hand for the picture. "The funny thing though is, this is how I always *recall* him (whenever I recall)—looking like this, I mean. So young and serious—not like he got to be. If he would have stayed this way, he'd be here right this minute. But Rosa, he changed. Folks all have to change, I know, but he didn't have no more will power than a flying squirrel. He didn't have nothing but the way he looked, and I never asked for nothing else, not in 1930 nohow. Then when the money got scarce as hens' back teeth and his drunks commenced coming so close they were one long drunk and he was sleeping nights wherever he dropped in fields or by the road—I took all that like a bluefaced fool. I never asked him once to change a thing till it was too late and he had filled me up with four big babies and himself to the brim with bootleg liquor and then walked into a pickup truck." She rubbed the picture on her dress for dust. "But like I said, I don't recall him that last way and I'm thankful."

Rosacoke said, "Who is the other boy?" (not bringing up her only recollection which was of that last way).

"I've been wondering too but I can't see his face. Maybe it was some little fellow they met that day and never saw again. Looks like he's hollering something, don't it?"

"Yes'm," she said. "Wonder what it was?"

But Mama was through with the picture. She thought it had served the purpose she meant it for, and she went to the mantel and propped it by the one of Wesley in uniform. "I'll leave it here for awhile so you can see it good. It'll be yours someday anyhow. None of the others wouldn't want it. That's why I didn't show it when I found it." Then she turned and said what she came to say. "Rosa, *he* ain't coming so why don't you get some good fresh air?"

Rosacoke faced the wall. "*He* ain't what I'm waiting for."

"Don't lie to me. What else is there but Judgment Day?"

"A heap of things, Mama." But she didn't name one. She lay in misery, wishing the Lord would strike her mother dumb, and far off a drone began and bore down nearer like some motorcycle leaning round curves to get to what it wants or like an arrow for her heart. She jumped off the bed and threw up the window and strained to see the road, but Baby Sister was dancing in the yard, pointing to the sky and screaming before the noise completely drowned her, "It's Willie, Rosacoke—make haste, it's Willie in the air!" And the shadow of Willie's fellow's plane, little as it was, swept over the yard and stirred the biggest oaks before it vanished north. When the drone passed over, Baby Sister was crying, "There's *three* folks in that plane!" And Mama said "There they go."

Rosacoke looked back to the mantel and the pictures and the mirror. "And here goes Rosacoke," she said. She put on a green winter dress and old easy shoes and didn't comb her hair that was tangled from misery. Her black Kodak was beside the photograph of her father with half a roll of summer pictures in it. She took it up and said, "I'm going to walk to Mary's. I told her I would take a picture of Mildred's baby to send to his aunts and uncles." Mama went over and spread up the bed and Rosacoke opened the door.

"You'll freeze like that," Mama said. So Rosacoke took her raincoat and a scarf like silk, and Mama said, "Walk easy down them steps. Milo and Sissie said they needed naps. You know what their naps are like— and Sissie big as a fifty-cent balloon."

Rosacoke heard that. She took off her shoes and shot past where Sissie and Milo were and on down the steps. In the downstairs hall she could hear Baby Sister through the porch door. That paper-doll mother was still mirating at her own flesh and blood having lice. Rosacoke smiled and thought, "That is the one funny thing since Heywood Betts and his Honolulu shirt." But thinking of him and Willie—and whoever else flew with them back to Norfolk—put her deep again in the misery she was running from so she stepped in her shoes and ran on—out the back and almost down the steps before she knew she was thirsty. She came up again to the porch where Milo had left the well-water he drew after dinner. She took one look at the 1937 New Jersey license her father nailed over the bucket, and she drank one dipper of water so cold every muscle in her throat gripped tight to stop her swallowing. But she swallowed and the new cold inside her seemed to ease the way she felt. She said, "I will just walk peaceful to Mary's and not think about a thing," and she started, walking quickly down the steps again and straight on ahead through four dead acres of purple cotton stalks and into a little pine woods that had one path. She walked with her head just level, not looking up where the plane had been or at anything else that would cause her to think. But Mary's was a mile from the Mustians', and a mile is right far to think about nothing.

Still she walked every step of that mile, and it was nearly four o'clock when she came to the end of the pines where Mary's was—three wood rooms and a roof, washed by the rain to no color at all, narrow and pointed sharp up from the packed white ground like a bone the sun sucked out when nothing else would grow. The only things that moved were brown smoke crawling from the chimney and a turkey that saw her at

once. Rosacoke stopped and said "Mary" as the turkey
was famous for temper. He gave a cocked look with his
raw red head and stepped away to let her pass. Mary
hadn't answered so Rosacoke climbed the steps and
said again "Mary" and opened the door. That was the
big low room where Mary slept, but there was no noise,
only dark and the smell of kerosene. Maybe they were
all at afternoon church. Rosacoke went in, thinking she
would leave a note to say she tried, but the only paper
in sight was magazine pages nailed to the wall to keep
out wind. Then she looked at the feather bed. In the
middle of it four pillows were boxed together like a
nest, and there was Mildred's baby laid on his back on
thick newspapers with fists clenched tight to his ears.
His head had twisted to the left, half buried in the
white pillow slip. The one cotton blanket was around
his feet where he had kicked it, and his dress which was
all he wore had worked up high on his chest, leaving
him bare to the chill of the day. Rosacoke went over
to him, thinking this meant Mary was somewhere near
and she should wait. When she saw the baby was deep
asleep, she bent low enough to hear him breathe. His
lips were shut and he breathed from all over—from the
awful top of his head where the skull left off and the
dark skin throbbed at anybody's mercy and from his
arched belly and the navel knobbing out almost as far
as what was underneath where the bud of him being a
boy crouched on the loaded sack and rose and fell
with the rest of him. He didn't seem cold but Rosacoke
thought she should cover him. She pulled at his dress
to get it down and raised the blanket gently from
around his feet. It was enough to jar his sleep. He
grunted high in his nose with his eyes still shut and
oared with his feet at the blanket and picked at his dress

with one slow hand. Rosacoke stood back—to keep him from seeing her if he woke—and prayed he wouldn't wake. His legs slowed down and the grunts, and for a minute he seemed asleep. Then he turned his head and opened his eyes on Rosacoke, and the scream he gave split out from whatever awful place he went to when he slept—describing it clear and wordless as a knife. Rosacoke thought of ways to quiet him, but they all meant picking him up—him screaming and naked again and her a stranger. He stared straight at her though, and even if he didn't see, she couldn't let him howl so again she pulled down his dress and reached under his head and back to lift him up, but he belched and thick yellow milk spewed down his neck into her hand. She jerked her hand as if it was scalded and flung the milk in clots on the floor and wiped her fingers quickly on Mary's bed. The screaming went on, but choked now and full. Rosacoke looked at the child and said, "Baby, *I* ain't what you need" and ran to the porch to try once more for Mary. This time Mary answered. "Here come Mary," she said, coming to the house from the privy, not smiling, taking her time.

Rosacoke said, "Come *on* then and help this baby."

"What you done to Mildred's baby, Miss Rosa?"

"Not a thing—but he's sick."

"He ain't sick, Miss Rosa. He just passing the time of day."

"Well, I went in to take his picture and he woke up."

"And you picked him up, didn't you, when I done just now fed him?" She still hadn't smiled.

"I was trying to hush him, Mary. Don't get mad."

"Yes'm. He throwed up his dinner, didn't he?"

"Yes."

Mary bent down for a leaf that lay on the spotless ground and studied it in her hand long enough for the turkey to creep up behind her, but she heard him and ran in his face—"Go on, sir!"—and he hobbled off. The screaming went on inside, a little tired now but steady, and Rosacoke frowned. Mary came slow up the steps, holding her straight back and said, "He throws up regular. I don't know if he can grow, not keeping hold of his nourishment no better."

"Go stop his crying, Mary."

"What you so scared of crying for? He come here crying and he be crying when I ain't here to hush him. He got his right to cry, Miss Rosa, and why ain't you used to babies by now?" Then she smiled and went in the door and said, "Come in, Miss Rosa. I'll get him clean and you take his picture."

But Rosacoke couldn't go back. She looked at the drained evening sky. "It's too dark now, I think. I better come back next Sunday."

Mary stopped in her tracks—"Yes'm, if that's what you think"—and Rosacoke went towards the pines. On the edge Mary called her back and gave her the Kodak she had left. Mary said, "They tell me Mr. Wesley got him a airplane."

"Who is *they*, Mary?"

"Estelle saw Mr. Wesley in the road last night, and he say he got him a eight-cylinder airplane to come home in and he was taking it to Norfolk this evening and to watch out for him in the sky."

"That won't Wesley's airplane, Mary. He just hitched a ride in it, and they have already gone back."

"Yes'm. How is he coming on, Miss Rosa?"

"I reckon he's fine. I ain't laid eyes on him since the funeral."

"Yes'm," Mary said, seeing how Rosacoke looked (though she held back half the misery from her face), seeing that was all she ought to say and watching Rosacoke head home again and stop and take another look at the sky.

"I'm going to see his Mama, Mary. Reckon she can tell me what I've done wrong?"

All Mary said was, "Step along fast, Miss Rosa, else night will catch you"—which the night was bound to do as the Beavers lived a good two miles further on, facing the road with their back to the woods that started at Mary's. She could walk home first and take the car and go by the road (it was three miles by the road), but that would mean explaining a lot to Mama and talking her way out of supper. If she walked on now through the woods, she could get to the Beavers' as they finished eating and do her talking and call for Milo to carry her home. So she crossed Mary's yard the other way, not seeing Mary still in the door, and passed into trees that gradually shielded out the baby's crying.

She had gone more than halfway before she was no longer running from Mildred's baby, and the trees had thinned to the place where a fire had been in the early spring, charring the sparse pines and opening the ground to the sky. She stopped there and wondered what she was running *to*—as if Wesley's mother knew how Wesley felt—and she thought of turning back. What could she say that the Beavers would understand? But turning back would put her in pitch dark in a little so she said to herself, "I will just walk on and ask the Beavers real nonchalant to let me use their phone and call Milo to pick me up. If they want to talk to me then, let *them* decide what to say." She took her breath to go, and a light wind in her face brought two things out to meet her—low on the trees a hawk with his tan wings locked to ride the air for hours (if the air would hold and the ground offer things to hunt) and his black eyes surely on her where she stood and clear against the sky, his iron beak, parting and meeting as he wheeled but giving no hawk sound—only shivering pieces of what seemed music riding under him that came and went with the breeze as if it was meant for nothing but the hawk to hear, as if it was made by the day for the hawk to travel with and help his hunting— yet frail and high for a killing bird and so faint and fleeting that Rosacoke strained on her toes to hear it better and cupped her ear, but the hawk saw that and his fine-boned wings met under him in a thrust so long and slow that Rosacoke wondered if they wouldn't touch *her*—his wings—and her lips fell open to greet him, but he was leaving, taking the music with him and the wind. She turned to watch him go and wanted to speak to call him back, but her lips moved silent as his beak. You could joke with a cardinal all day long, but what did you say to something like a hawk?— nothing that a hawk would answer so she just went on, helped by the breeze that pushed from behind her now, not practicing things she could say to the Beavers nor the way she would try to look, but searching her mind to name what pieces of music the hawk carried with him and wondering what had made them. But the memory was fainter already than the music, and it hung in her mind, unfinished and alone, spreading its curious sadness over whatever troubles she had, burying them deeper than feeling and frowning, leaving her

free for this short space in evening air that was warm
for early November with the last light clung to the
slope of her cheek where colorless down, too soft to see
in the day, swirled up to her temple and the coarse yellow hair laid back on the flickering wind and her legs
pumped on through weeds that were dead already
from the frosts but still were green and straight—free
to go on or back while she took the last few steps that
put her nearly in sight of the Beavers'. Then the wind
turned round once more, and the music was on it, close
and whole. Now there was no going back because it
was Wesley, sure as war would come, playing his Navy
harmonica when she had counted on him being in
Norfolk or at least headed north in Willie Duke's plane.

The Beavers' house sat back from the road at a
slant and in a white dirt clearing but with trees reaching round on three sides like arms to the road. When
Rosacoke came to the end of the trees, she could have
seen the side of the house, but she circled just out of
sight till she was almost at the road. Then she turned
and there was the porch, fifty yards away, and the three
steps and on the top step, Wesley's youngest brother
Claude, sitting on his hands, looking to where Wesley
was, hearing the music.

Wesley was on his feet at the corner of the porch
nearest Rosacoke, leaning one shoulder on the last
post, facing the road but looking down. From the trees
Rosacoke could see three-fourths of him—the dark blue
trousers he had worn all summer, the loose white shirt,
his hair lighter from the sun at Ocean View—all but his
face. He covered most of that with his hands that
quivered tight on the harmonica till the music stopped
for awhile. Then one hand opened and it started again
—not songs or tunes and like nothing she had known

since she was a girl and heard old Negroes blowing
harps as if they remembered Africa and had been grand
kings or like Milo that summer he grew up (when his
beard arrived, the color of broomstraw) and went past
telling her his business and every evening sat in the
dusk after supper before he would leave the house,
whistling out his secrets in tunes she never understood
and planning back of his eyes what he would do with
the night when it fell altogether (which would be to
walk three miles to see an Abbott girl who was older
than him—and an orphan that lived with her uncle—
and was taking him in dark tobacco barns, teaching him
things too early that some folks never learn). Anyhow,
it was nothing *she* had ever sung to him—something
else he learned away from home, maybe in the Navy.
("But if the Navy is sad as that," she thought, "why do
folks join it of their own free will?")

In all she could see—the yard, the house, his
brother, him, the trees beyond—his hands were the
only moving things. The wind had died completely,
his brother watched him as still as she did, and Wesley
himself was still as a blind man when his guide suddenly leaves him, embedded upright in the gray air like
a fish in winter, frozen in the graceful act, locked in
the ice and staring up with flat bitter eyes—far out as
anything can be and come back. But his hands *did*
move—them and the music—to show he could leave
any minute if leaving was what he wanted. (How could
she know what he wanted?) And his brother spoke—
or moved his mouth. Like that boy in the picture with
her father (him on the left, holding up like a lily the
American flag, speaking silence to the wind), she
couldn't make out the sound but Wesley could. He
took down his hands and looked at his brother and

laughed and said "No" to whatever the question was, and they talked on awhile, too quiet for her to hear but with enough laughing to make Wesley roll his head so she could see. "He just don't know," she thought. "He don't know how he looks." Then the talking stopped and Claude went in the house. Wesley hesitated a minute, knocking the harmonica on his hand and looking to the road as if Rosacoke, unseen, had made him think of leaving. "There ought to be a way," she thought. "There ought to be some way you could hold him there. Anybody who looks like that—you ought to give them anything you have. Anything you have and they want *bad* enough." So she went on towards him and thought of nothing but that.

And from the moment she broke through the trees, he watched her come, stepping long as she always did, not showing a thing he hadn't seen a thousand times before. She was watching the ground which meant she was deciding the first word to say, and that meant Wesley didn't have any cause for worry. Not meaning to play but for something to do, he raised the harmonica again, and when she got to the steps and looked up at him, he smiled from behind his hands.

"I heard you playing," she said and pointed behind her to the woods. "I have been to Mary's to take that baby's picture, but he was scared of me, and I thought I would just take a walk to here—it being so warm—and call up Milo to come get me. A half a mile back I heard you playing. But I didn't know it was you. I thought you were air-borne by now." She grinned and his answering laugh whined through the harmonica and made her say, "If you managed everything good as you manage a harp, wouldn't none of your friends ever be upset."

"I never studied it," he said, "—harp-playing, I mean. Just what I picked up in Norfolk."

"That's where I reckoned you were tonight—else I wouldn't be standing here."

"I got tomorrow off," he said.

"There were three folks in that plane going back."

"I know that," he said. "I surrendered my seat to Willie's Mama. Anyhow, I won't riding back with Heywood Betts. He drives a airplane about as good as I tap-dance. I been laid up airsick till this evening."

"Have you? Mary said Estelle saw you in the road last night."

"Yes she did," he said and tightened his lips, not as if he had made a joke but as if he had ridden that track as far as he intended and wouldn't she like to throw the switch?

"Well, can I use the phone?" she said. "I better be calling Milo so they won't think I have died."

"I can carry you home."

"Thank you but my stomach hasn't been real easy lately, and I won't trust it to a motorcycle ride tonight."

"The motorcycle is in Norfolk. You didn't think I brought it down here in a airplane, did you?"

"Do me a favor," she said. "Say *Rosacoke*."

"Why?"

"Just say it please."

He said "Rosacoke" like an answer for a doctor that asked to see his tonsils.

"Thank you," she said. "That is my name. I bet you ain't said it since late July."

"I don't walk around talking to trees and shrubs like some folks if that's what you mean."

"That's not what I mean but never mind. You are Wesley—is that still right?"

"Unless the Law has changed it and not notified *me*."

"I was just checking. I know such a few facts about you and your doings that sometimes I wonder if I even know your right name."

"Yes ma'm. You can rest easy on that. It's Wesley all right and is Wesley riding you home or ain't he?—because if he is, he will have to get the keys."

"If nobody else is wanting the car, I'd thank you," she said, thinking her last chance might be coming, thinking she might find the way to give him whatever he wanted to calm him down—thinking she knew what he wanted. She would do her best but maybe Wesley didn't want anything she had, not any more. "He must give a sign first," she said to herself, and when he went for the keys, she made up what the sign would be. There were two ways Wesley could turn when they got to the road, and the way he turned would be the sign. If he went right—that was the bad road but the quickest—they would ride all the way past dead open fields and be at Rosacoke's in no time. But if he turned left—that was the long circle way that would take them first through an arched mile of trees and then past Mount Moriah and Mr. Isaac's bottomless woods where the spring was and the deer had been and, beyond, Delight Church and the pond and the Mustians'.

Wesley came out of the back yard in the tan Pontiac with no lights on and waited while she got in. It was full night but they coasted down the drive in darkness like thieves and stopped when they came to the road. Then Wesley turned on the bright lights, and the car headed left slow as if it turned itself. That was the sign and Rosacoke waited for what would come after.

But they ran through the darkest mile in silence with Wesley gripping both hands to the wheel and watching the road like foreign country and Rosacoke catching little glimpses of him in the dashboard light as he passed up every chance to slow down or stop—ruts and holes and even the hidden turn-in that had been his favorite stopping place when she first knew him, where they had sat many an hour other nights (not talking much, to be sure, not needing talk then), and on past Mount Moriah, lit up and full of black singing, and when that died behind them and they commenced the first long curve of Mr. Isaac's woods, Rosacoke said, "I might as well be behind you on the motorcycle for all the talking we have done."

"What do you want to say?"

"Wesley, you are at least half of this trouble, and you said you would *talk*. In that last letter you said I was getting you out of your writing depth and hadn't we better talk when you got home."

"I don't remember everything I say in letters."

"Well, I sure to God do. I learn them by heart just trying to figure out what you mean."

"God A-mighty, Rosa, I don't mean *nothing* by them. I just say whatever—" but they had pulled round that first curve, and the headlights shot forward unblocked. Wesley said "Sweet Jesus" and Rosacoke said "Stop" because their light struck a deer the moment it flung from the woods on the right, broadside to them in the air with its hair still red for summer and the white brush of its tail high and stiff, holding in the leap for the time it took to see them coming, then heaving its head and twisting the leap back on itself to where it started in the dark—before they could speak again. But when it was gone (from their eyes, not their minds) with crashing enough for a herd, Wesley stopped where they were and said, "He is the first one I ever seen try it."

"Try what?"

"Try to get his does across the road to water, I guess. It ain't too late for that."

"Was it a buck then?"

"Didn't you see his horns?"

"I guess I did—he was so sudden." They sat on, still, a moment. Then Wesley reached for the gears, and quick as gunfire Rosacoke said, "I saw one once before way behind Mr. Isaac's spring—Mildred and me, nine years ago. It wouldn't have been this same one, would it?"

"Not hardly," he said and the car didn't move.

"What water would he be taking them to—the spring?"

"Not hardly—that'll be clogged up—but there's creeks all back in there if you go far enough."

Those were the most peaceful words they had said since late July. Rosacoke took them as one more sign and saw a way to keep them going. "Reckon will he try to cross them over again?"

"I reckon so if he don't see no more lights for awhile. He's watching us right now from somewhere back there, waiting till we go."

"Pity we can't see them cross," she said.

"He may not try again right here, but we can wait up yonder in the tracks to the spring if you ain't in a hurry."

She knew Mama and Milo would already be standing on their heads with worry, but she said, "I can wait. All I got to do is go to work at nine o'clock in the morning."

Wesley turned off the lights and when his eyes had set to the dark, there was a little moon to show him the grown-over tracks just ahead that used to lead Mr. Isaac to his spring. He eased the car towards them and backed in to face the road. He pulled up the brake and lowered his window and leaned his arms on the top of the wheel and pressed his forehead on the glass to see the trees beyond the road and whatever they held. Rosacoke reckoned that was a temporary position— that in a minute he would move in as far as she let him. To pass the time she looked ahead too, but not the way Wesley did. He *only* waited—nothing else crossed his mind but seeing that deer and how many does he would have. Rosacoke thought, "Him and that deer are something similar. Not but a few things wait like they do. Most things are busy hunting"—she thought that last so clearly she couldn't swear to not saying it. But if she said it Wesley just waited harder. He didn't move. So she closed her eyes for the next thinking to begin, but a picture came instead—of that cool November day seven years ago and the path and the pecan tree with Wesley up it like an eagle shaking down nuts at her request, not hungry enough to want them himself —old enough though to want *her* (other boys that young had wanted her) but not even caring enough to ask her name, much less for anything better, just waiting nicely till she left him alone with what he could see from the fork he stood in, sweeping nearly all Warren County with his eyes and telling her he saw smoke to make her leave—and him so hard to leave even then with the threat of being grown hung on him like thunder. With her eyes still closed she ran through all her time with Wesley till finally she could say to herself, "Mama lived with my Daddy fifteen years and took his babies and his drunks, and now she don't recall him but as a little serious boy in a picture. That is the way I recollect Wesley—like that first November day. Every other way is like that—him waiting for something to happen to *him*, daring somebody to do something nice such as come up and touch him just so he could say, 'Why in the world did you do *that?*' and hold on tight till whoever bothered him vanished—and nothing about him since has ever surprised me. I knew from the first, young as I was, what was coming. Take a child like Mildred's—you can look at him and say if he is a pretty or ugly *child*. You can't see what he will look like when he is grown though. But that first time—wasn't Wesley standing plain as day in a clear shadow of his grown man's body that sat out around him like a boundary he had to fill? *I* saw it and young as I was, I saw there wasn't no room for Rosacoke Mustian in what *that* boy would turn out to be. So he went on filling out his boundary lines and getting the face I knew he would, and while he was getting it, he came to me all those times and I let him have me to kiss and touch, and I said to myself, 'He has changed and this is love.' But all those times I was no more to him than water to a boat—just a thing he was using to get somewhere on, to get *grown* so he could tear off to Norfolk, Virginia and the U.S. Navy and every hot hussy that would stretch out under him and tell him 'Yes' where I said 'No.' And just because of that Rosacoke went out of his mind completely. I knew from the first it would happen, but that didn't make no difference. I hoped he would change but he didn't change, and *that* didn't make no difference." She said it out loud—"Wesley, do you reckon on ever changing any?"

He didn't look round. He whispered gently as if he was asking a favor, "Rosa, no deer is going to walk in on a round-table discussion of Wesley Beavers' personality."

"Yes sir," she said but she had thought all she needed to think. She had made herself see what she had to do. So she waited—not to see the deer and his does but knowing if they crossed to water, they would be her chance to save Wesley from running off again. She waited by staring at her dark lap and her hands that lay flat and nearly unseen on her flanks.

And they crossed—the deer, a little above where the buck had showed before. She didn't see their first steps or hear them, so dainty on the packed road, till she felt Wesley's whole body stiffen forward—not by him touching her but through the springs of the seat. She looked to where his brow pressed hard on the glass and turned herself along his gaze to where she caught them the moment they sank into Mr. Isaac's woods—three deer moving careful as clock wheels so close together she couldn't see which was the buck and was leading. But they drew her on behind them. Wesley felt that too (he had seen them longer than she), and he strained so hard to see their last that she whispered, "There's safety glass between them and you, Wesley, and you are about to poke your head right through it." But when the deer were gone, Wesley gave no sign of taking the chance they offered. He only said, "Now you have seen two does getting led to water" and reached for the key to crank the motor.

Rosacoke laid her hand on his wrist. "Since it's a warm night how come we don't wait and walk in behind them and see is it the spring they are after?"

He looked at her hand, not her, and saw what she meant. "If you want to," he said, "but we ain't coming near that buck."

"If we went gentle maybe we could."

Wesley reached in the back seat for a flashlight and opened his door. He came to her side and stood while she got out. They walked a few loud steps through weeds that were dead from the frosts and then struck into the trees with hands at their sides, separate and not swinging till they walked so close their fingers brushed and their hands went together so natural you couldn't say who took whose. Then the walking was quiet because there was pine straw under their feet and darker because they were under black pines and Wesley didn't once switch on his light. It was early November and the snakes were gone. They knew the path. And they both knew where they were headed—which wasn't to the spring because when they came to the spring and Rosacoke held back on his hand (thinking she should mention deer) and whispered "Are they there?" Wesley just breathed out through his nose to show he had laughed (he was too dark to see), and Rosacoke said, "Throw your light on the spring and see is it clean," but he led her on where the path gave way to the thickness of leaves and soft old logs that powdered beneath their feet and the deer passed out of their minds completely, and Rosacoke thought of nothing but "Where will we stop?" till a briar bush stopped them. Wesley was one step ahead when the briars took hold, and Rosacoke walked up against him. That was when the light came on (Wesley must have done it but without a sound) and showed them piece of a broomstraw field. Wesley pulled out of the bush, and the light went off without them seeing each other. They walked on hip-deep in straw another few yards before any sound was made. Rosacoke said, "Don't let's go no farther" and they stopped again. "Listen," she said.

They listened awhile. Then he said "Listen to what?"

"I thought we might hear them," she said. "It was a field like this where Mildred and me saw that other deer."

"It wasn't this field," he said.

"How come it wasn't?"

"This is my private field. Mr. Isaac don't know he owns this field. Don't *nobody* know this field but me."

"I never knew it," she said, "and I been walking these woods my whole life."

"You know it now."

She said "Yes I do" but she couldn't see it. She couldn't see at all. She thought she was facing Wesley though nothing but her seemed to breathe, and she thought they were standing on level ground. Her left hand was still in those other hard fingers, but when she offered her right hand, she only touched straw that sighed. She drew back in sudden terror and said to herself, "I don't even know this is Wesley. I have not laid eyes on his face since we left the car." So she spoke again, calm as she could—"Would you switch on the light so I can see your field?"

"You ain't aiming to take no pictures, are you?" He was facing her and he sounded like Wesley, but from that minute on, she wouldn't have sworn just who she was giving up to.

"I left my Kodak in the car," she said. "It don't work at night."

"Then if you don't need no light, I surely don't," he said and took her other hand and pulled her gentle under him to the ground. The straw lay down where they were and stood up wherever they weren't, and Rosacoke reached behind her head to grip her hands in its dryness. The last clear thought she had was, "If it was light it would all be the color of Milo's beard."

But Wesley didn't need any light. He started above her and even if the sun had poured all over him, she couldn't have seen the one thing she needed to see, which was down to where he was locked already at the center of what she had started, where he was maybe alone or, worse than that, keeping company in the dark with whatever pictures his mind threw up—of some other place he would rather be or some girl he knew that was better. But he didn't speak to tell her *where* he was. He only moved and even that was a way he never had moved in all the evenings she had known him—from inside the way he did everything but planned this time fine as any geared wheel, slow at first and smooth as your eyeball under the lid, no harder than rocking a chair and touching her only in that new place, but soon taking heart and oaring her as if he was nothing but the loveliest boat on earth and she was the sea that took him where he had to go, and then multiplying into what seemed a dozen boys swarming on her with that many hands and mouths and that many high little whines coming up to their lips that were nothing like words till the end when they came so close they broke out in one long "Yes," and what he had made, so careful, fell in like ruins on them both, and all she had left was her hands full of broomstraw and one boy again, dead-weight on her body, who whispered to her softer than ever, "I thank you, Mae" (which wasn't any part of her name) and not knowing what he had said, rolled off her and straightaway threw his flashlight on the sky. The beam rose up unstopped and she turned away to keep him from seeing the things he had done to her face—the look he had left there. But he didn't notice. All the light went up and he studied that awhile. Then he said, "Did you know this light won't never stop flying?" She didn't answer so he laid the back of his hand on some part of her that was dry as peach-skin still and said, "There ain't a thing to block it. It'll be flinging on when you and me are olden times."

But now that their moving had stopped, the chill of the night set in, and Rosacoke shuddered beneath his hand before she said, "Is that something else you learned in the Navy?"

"Yes'm," he said. "Ain't I a good learner?" And with his hand he asked again for what she had given so free before but she held him back.

"Why?" he said, thinking naturally he had the right.

"I got to go home."

"What you got at home that's half as good as what I got right here?" He pulled her hand through the dark to where he was ready.

But her hand was dead in his. She drew it away and he heard her stand. "If you aren't carrying me back, I will have to walk, but since you know these woods so good, please lend me your flashlight."

He threw the beam on her face and said "Sweet Jesus" to what he saw—which was no Rosacoke he had seen before. She looked straight down at his light, not seeing him behind it, not hiding any more. Then she opened her mouth, thinking only if she could speak, the hate on her face would break into something gentler like regret. But all she could do was hunch her shoulders, and if Wesley in the Navy had sometimes forgot how she looked, he wouldn't forget again.

"Are you all right?" he said.

"I'm all right," she said and started for the road.

Wesley had some dressing to do before he could follow so Rosacoke walked to the edge where the briars began and waited while he caught up behind her with the light. When he was two steps away and the light spread round her feet, she moved on again, not slowing once and with every step, her front leg striding from her raincoat just beyond his light as if she couldn't bear *its* touch either. Wesley let her go that way till the path widened out where the spring should be. Then he came up beside her and said, "How about us stopping a minute to see is the deer been stirring the spring?" and he laid his arm along her back.

"You ain't studying deer," she said and ran on to the car.

Not knowing whether she would wait or walk on home, Wesley took his time. He walked to the spring and shined his light down in it. The deer hadn't passed that way, hadn't stopped anyhow. The vines were in place. The water was clear and the bottom was clean—most likely since the day of Mildred's funeral. But there was one broken stick, half in, half out. The underwater half was furred with tan sediment, and on the black half above was a single ugly moth, the color of the sediment. It was still—the moth—and Wesley knelt to touch it and see was it dead, but it took a little bothered flight and settled on the stick again. It had lasted two frosts so he let it sleep, and since he was kneeling he bent all the way and laid his mouth to the spring and drew three swallows of water. Then he stood and said to himself, "It will run on clean another two weeks. Then the leaves will take over."

He had taken his time because he thought he knew what Rosacoke's trouble was and—if she had waited—how to ease her. And when he got to the car, she had waited. She had also straightened her hair, but her face was the same so he drove that last little way in silence. Not a frog was left in the pond nor a dryfly in the trees, and the nearest noise was the singing at Mount Moriah (if they were still singing), but that was behind them now, and Rosacoke gave no sign of wanting the talk she asked for before. She watched the road. But Wesley had one thing to say which he thought was gentle and which he thought she needed, and when he turned in the Mustians' drive, he stopped under their big pecan tree and said it. "Rosa, you got to remember that the way you feel is a natural thing after what we done. It'll pass on off in a little, and you'll feel good as you ever did. I guarantee that. And if we was to do it again sometime, it wouldn't last nearly as long—you feeling sad, I mean, about what we done."

"*We* ain't done nothing, Wesley—" She might have explained if they hadn't heard the front door slam. The porch light was off but what they saw was bound to be Milo coming towards them. He stopped halfway, just looking at the car, and Rosacoke said, "I got to go. He's worried about me."

"He ain't worried now," Wesley said. "He knows this car." And Rosacoke might have believed him and sat awhile if Sissie inside hadn't just then switched on the light and stepped on the porch and stood. The light didn't reach out quite to the car, but it struck along Milo's back—him facing them with his hands at his sides, working, and his head all dark but his hair lit up.

"I'm going," she said and opened her door. She was out on the ground before he could move, and she whispered, "Now leave here fast. Milo is mad at you anyhow, and I don't want him seeing your face."

"Well, are you all right?"

"I'm all right. I was just mistaken. But so were you—my name hasn't never been Mae." And before he could open his mouth, she had walked off towards Milo, standing with the light against his hair (his hair the color it was). When she came close enough to show her face, *he* would know why she looked the way she did. He wouldn't speak of it to her or sing his advice again. He would just walk in behind her. But later in the night (in bed when he got chilly) wouldn't he roll over on Sissie his wife and tell her what he knew? Which would make four people that knew—Rosacoke herself and Wesley Beavers and Milo her brother and Sissie Abbott his wife who was big as a fifty-cent balloon.

MONDAY afternoon was clear and cold, and Wesley hitched himself to Norfolk, not seeing Rosacoke again. But that weekend he sent this letter.

November 10

Dear Rosa,

It is way past time good boys was all in the bed but I am still up so will just write a line to say I'm back on the job. (I was last week, I mean, which don't signify I'll be there tomorrow if I wake up feeling like I expect to.) Also I am writing to know wouldn't you like to come up here Thanksgiving if you get any time off? The reason I ask is I won't be coming home again before Xmas as the only time I have off is Thanksgiving and some folks I know are throwing a big party that weekend. A lot of my friends have left for good. That's what living in a Navy town means. But there is enough left to keep the ball rolling so why don't you come on up for the holidays? You could stay at your Aunt Oma's or I could get you a room in the boarding house where I stay—that would suit me better.

What's suiting me right now though is my bed that's waiting so good night Rosa. Say hello to everybody for me. I'm sorry I didn't see Milo. What did you mean about him being mad at me? I'm hoping I'll hear from you soon and see you in a little. Hoping also you have got over your blues from last Sunday evening, I am

Yours for a good night's sleep,
Wesley

Two evenings later when Rosacoke came home from work, Baby Sister ran out to meet her. She said,

"Guess where you got a letter from?" But Rosacoke didn't ask. She walked straight to the living room and spoke to Milo who was nodding but who woke up to watch her read the letter. It was propped on the mantel, but Rosacoke waited, warming her hands at the stove. When she finally looked and saw Wesley's writing, she took it and started upstairs. Baby Sister said, "You don't have to go in the freezer to read it!" (meaning there were no fires lit upstairs), but Rosacoke went and turned on the one ceiling light and lay on her bed with the letter in her hand, wishing she never had to open it, knowing—whatever it said—it would call on her for some awful answer. When she read his first line, she knew what the answer was and wrote it out then.

November 12

Dear Wesley,

No my blues are not over. What makes you think they ought to be? Everybody in the world doesn't feel the same as you. I don't think I have ever felt the same as you about anything except the weather—even then you don't sweat when it's hot—and sure thing I don't feel like spending my little Thanksgiving on a Greyhound bus bumping back and forth to Norfolk so I can tag behind you to a party full of folks I don't know and wouldn't want to know if I met them, including Mae. Anyhow Mama and Aunt Oma are not on speaking terms so I couldn't stay there and thank you very much but I won't be boarding at your place either. I have been deer-hunting once already and once was enough for me.

Sincerely,
Rosacoke

She addressed it and stood it on her own mantel by the picture of her father as a boy—where the one of Wesley had been. But she didn't seal it. Her habit was to let letters cool overnight and read them one more time in the morning. And in the morning she tore it up, not because what she said was wrong but because maybe she should wait. How could you just say "No" that way after waiting six years to say "Yes"?

She waited five days but nothing changed really—not for her, not inside—so on Saturday night she sat down in the kitchen to write again, not thinking what she would finally say or how, not knowing how she really felt, but thinking maybe things might change the way Wesley said if she just wrote the news of that bad week and put Wesley's name at the top.

November 16

Dear Wesley,

Thanking you for your letter that I'm sorry to take so long to answer but we are having a right busy week here, especially as Sissie has been having her baby on and off for the last two nights and all day today. No seriously, she started up Friday evening—yesterday. She was three days overdue yesterday. And those three days have been a real experience for all of us—the evenings anyway with nothing to do but sit and watch Milo trying to cheer up Sissie. We got through the first two evenings somehow till Milo finally said he was tired and took Sissie off to sleep (they have been sleeping downstairs in Mama's room for ten days in case of emergency) and we started last night as usual—Sissie had spent most of the day lying down but rose up at sunset to eat with us. When we got through that I volunteered to wash dishes and the others went on in the living room. I took my time in the kitchen but when I couldn't find another thing to wash, I joined them. Baby Sister was just finishing her part of the entertainment—a description of her wedding plans (age 12, just dreaming). She had got as far as the music arrangements. All the music she wants is "Kiss of Fire" and alot of Gupton children laying down pine cones in her path. I sat down and took up my knitting (I am knitting Sissie a bed jacket) which was the signal for Milo to make his remark about what a dangerous thing it was making Sissie a bed jacket because once Sissie got down didn't we know how hard it would be ever to get her up? (The truth. Last winter she reacted to roseola like it was pellagra.) We laughed some at that, even Sissie who has been more sensitive than usual lately (setting a new world's record). Then there was a lull and everybody stared at their own lap, glad of a few minutes peace. But it didn't last. Sissie gave a little moan and lurched in her chair to show the baby had just rearranged itself. Milo said, "Is he traveling again?" (Milo knows it's a boy) and Mama said, "He must be hungry" and stood up and said she would serve the dessert now—we had all been too full after supper. So she went off and came back with cherry Jello which we have eaten right much of lately, it being what Sissie craves—lucky she craves something cheap—and while we were eating that, somebody knocked on the door. It was Macey Gupton and Arnold his brother (the bachelor with no palate that you may never have seen—they don't show him off much). Macey and Mama are both deacons at Delight and they are the committee to select the gift the church will give Mr. Isaac at the Christmas pageant when he retires as Chairman of the Board of Deacons and Macey had come by to say he was driving up to Raleigh on Saturday and would get the gift if they could decide what it ought to be. Milo met them at the door and invited them in like prodigal sons—so happy to see anybody that might bring Sissie cheerful relief, much less Macey Gupton who had sat by and seen Marise have baby after baby like puppies. So they came in and took their seats. Arnold took a rocker as far out from everybody as he could get—it was like having Rato back. They had Jello and then everybody commenced asking what to get Mr. Isaac. Macey said didn't we think it ought to be something useful? There was discussion on that but nobody came up with anything that would be any real use to Mr. Isaac in his condition. Milo said, "Get him a wife. That is what he has needed all these years"—and asked Arnold if that wasn't so. Arnold just grinned and kept on rocking but Macey said he was serious and was thinking of something big like a wheel chair to replace that leather one Sammy totes. Milo said, "Hold on. What does a rolling chair cost?" Macey said, "Alot but we could collect a little from every member." Milo said, "Do you realize, Macey, that if Mr. Isaac wanted a rolling chair, he could buy a sterling silver one easy as you and I can buy a cigar?" Mama said that was the truth and that she thought it would just upset Mr. Isaac to spend so much on him now so late in life. Milo said, "Yes and do you know what he'd rather have than anything you could give him?—a sack of horehound candy." Everybody laughed, knowing it was true—it is what we give him every Christmas—and seeing he had hit a snag with his rolling chair, Macey changed the subject. He looked over at Sissie ramrodded in her chair (nobody had looked at her since the Guptons arrived) and said,

"Well when is it going to be?" Sissie said, "It ought to been three days ago." Mama said that was just the doctor's guess—that it would come when it got ready. And Milo said, "Ready or not, he better hurry up. He's got to make room for the other nine." He asked Sissie if that wasn't so. She said it could be if he would do the having. Macey said children were like socks—you couldn't have too many and if you did you could have a rummage sale with the surplus—but he wondered if they hadn't started right late. Milo said, "No. I timed it beautiful. He is coming just in time for the pageant." (This year is Sissie's turn to be Mary and Milo keeps saying she can use their boy for Jesus.) But Sissie said, "Kiss my foot. You are not timing this baby and don't be a fool about Christmas. Even if I have this baby and am well enough to be Mary, I am not taking it out in the December night at age six weeks to be Baby Jesus or anybody else." Macey looked back at her and said, "Smile, honey. You haven't got nothing to worry about. You are built very much like Marise and Marise has babies like a Indian-lady." I had been watching Sissie through the whole discussion and I knew the end of the rope was coming soon. Well it came right then— Sissie stood up quicker than she had done anything for weeks and said, "I may be big as a house but Marise Gupton is one thing I am not" *and then walked out and on upstairs before any of us could stop her, stairs being the last thing she should have climbed. Mama and Milo went up behind her, leaving me and Baby Sister alone with the Guptons to smooth over Sissie's performance. I said a few excusing things such as "Poor Sissie, her nerves are skinned bare with waiting" but my heart wasn't in it and naturally Macey felt uneasy at touching off the scene. He sat there pecking*

*his teeth and listening to hear Sissie bellow and Arnold
just rocked faster and faster till he rocked up nerve to
say he was sleepy and how come they didn't leave?
Macey looked like he wanted to—by the nearest exit—
but he felt compelled to stay till somebody came down
and reported on Sissie so we sat on in silence till
Milo arrived to say she was resting though not speaking, which would do her good, and for everybody to
sit still and we could play a little Setback. Everybody
sat and Milo was getting out the card table when
Mama came in. He asked her, "Has she had it?" Mama
took a look at the card table and said, "No and playing
cards under her isn't going to make it come easier."
But Milo went on setting up the table and then
looked round. I could see right away what the next
problem would be. Milo said, "Arnold, can you play?"
Arnold said "Yes" and Milo said, "Who is going to
hold the fourth hand?" Baby Sister volunteered but
Mama said, "No ma'm. Sit still." So Milo looked at
me and rather than let the evening fall through any
further, I said I would. Well we played. Milo and I
were partners against the Guptons and I wish you
could have seen us. Arnold cheated like we were playing for lives which of course meant they won time after
time but that didn't matter. We were just helping the
clock go round and when it had gone to about 9:30,
I could see Milo was tired of playing. He asked Mama
(who had sat there and smiled at Arnold's cheating
like it was a judgment on us all) if she wasn't planning
to serve something to our company? She said there
wasn't a thing but more Jello though it would be a
different flavor. Arnold asked if she had a few cold
biscuits and some syrup but there wasn't a biscuit in
the house so everybody took Jello and just as we*

started eating, Macey said we ought to get back to deciding on Mr. Isaac's gift. Milo said, "First let me just see does Sissie want some of this" and went to the foot of the steps and hollered to her. We all listened and there was no answer so Milo, instead of climbing the stairs like a human being, said louder, "Sissie, do you want to come down and eat some nice Jello with us?" From behind closed doors, Sissie said "No"—loud. Milo turned round to rejoin us but just as he stepped in the door, Sissie followed her "No" with a yell that turned into "Mama"—she mostly calls Mama Mrs. Mustian. Milo went white and said "Mama, you go." Mama said "Come on, Rosa" and I followed her, knowing I could be no help. Sissie was lying there scared to death and crying easy so as not to upset whatever would happen next. Mama sat down by her and started soothing and told me to call Dr. Sledge and tell him the waters had broke (if you know what that means). I went down to call and Milo was waiting at the steps to know was Sissie dead. I told him live and then called Dr. Sledge and told him what Mama said. He asked me alot of questions but I couldn't answer any of them and he said in that case, he would be out as soon as he could. Milo had gone upstairs while I was on the phone and when I hung up, Macey was standing behind me. He had heard what I said and just wanted to tell me it was nothing to worry about. I said I was glad to hear it and hoped everything would be over soon, meaning that as a hint for him and Arnold to leave, but he said, "Sometimes it don't come for a day or so after this"—and walked back in the living room to wait for Milo. I knew I would be all thumbs upstairs so I followed Macey and took a seat. Macey of course wanted to discuss having babies and how Marise did it but Baby Sister was right there on the piano bench which put a damper on him. It wasn't till he gave up trying though that we all missed Arnold. He was gone from his rocker and didn't answer when Macey called his name so Macey went looking for him and came back in a little to say he was sitting out in their truck in the cold—scared and saying he wouldn't come back in. "He'll freeze solid out there," I said and Macey said, "Yes I'm fixing to take him home but I'll come right back in case you all need any help from an Old Hand." There was nothing to say but "All right." Macey was looking forward to a Setting-Up more than I was, especially as I was the one person present who had to work Saturday morning but anyhow he went on off to put Arnold to sleep and Baby Sister said why didn't she and I make some candy so we did that—fudge, and before we got it in the refrigerator, Dr. Sledge came. He examined Sissie and said exactly what Macey had said—nothing bad had happened and things had more or less started but they might not end for a day or more. He sat awhile with Sissie to ease her mind. Then he came down and we gave him some of our candy and while he was eating it, Macey returned, bringing best wishes from Marise. Dr. Sledge asked Macey what was he doing here and Macey said he had come for the Setting-Up. Dr. Sledge said, "I thought you had enough of those at your place" and he and Macey commenced expert talk about when it would come. Dr. Sledge said he had no idea it would be before morning and he would just have to leave and see a few people that were bad off. Then he asked me to step out and call Milo and when Milo came down, he repeated all that to him. Milo of course wasn't happy at him leaving but Dr. Sledge said there

*wasn't a thing he could do for Sissie till pains started
and when they did, there would be plenty of time for
him to get here. So Milo resigned himself and said,
"Macey, you'll stay with me, won't you?" Macey said
"Sure" and Dr. Sledge went up to say a few soothing
things to Sissie before he left. I wish he had said a few
more to Milo because the minute he walked out the
door, Milo commenced twitching—and not a thing to
worry about with Sissie resting easy and Mama sitting
beside her, knowing all she knew about babies—but
he got worse and worse till Macey said, "What we
ought to do is just get Mary Sutton to come spend the
night." (She has midwifed all her life and helped all
of us get born.) That suited Milo fine so he and
Macey took off by foot to get Mary, not saying a word
to Mama or Sissie. Things were quiet the whole long
time they were gone but when they came back, Mary
was with them and she had brought Mildred's baby with
her (Estelle not being home to keep him). She had put
blankets in a cardboard box and laid him in that and
when she got to our place, she set the box down near
the woodstove in the kitchen and went upstairs to see
Sissie. Just having Mary in the house seemed to settle
Milo's nerves and he and Macey took seats in the living
room and went on talking. Baby Sister and I stayed in
the kitchen. By then it was nearly midnight and things
being so relieved with Mary here, I was thinking mostly
of how soon working time would come and Baby
Sister was getting wall-eyed from lack of sleep so I told
her to go on in Mama's room and stretch out there and
I would join her in a little. (She was scared of going
upstairs where Sissie was.) She asked me to wake her
up when it came which I promised to do and then she
went, leaving me in the kitchen with nothing but*

*Mildred's baby and him doing nothing but breathing
in his sleep, laid back in his box, the color of Mildred.
(They are just calling him Sledge. I still haven't
heard what the last name is, if any.) And sitting at the
kitchen table with the room so warm and no noise
but what laughing came through from Milo and
Macey, I nodded off and didn't wake up till after
2 a.m. when Mary tipped in to feed Sledge. He hadn't
cried. She had just waked him up and given him the
bottle and he was half-done when I came to. Mary said
Sissie was asleep and Milo and Macey were nodding in
the living room so why didn't I go on to bed? I
watched her put Sledge down and then I went in
Mama's room with Baby Sister and slept like death till
Mama shook me at 6:30. She beckoned me into the
kitchen and asked me was I going to work? I said,
"Not if you need me here" and she said there wouldn't
be a thing I could do now that Mary was here so I told
her to stretch out by Baby Sister and gather her
strength (she hadn't shut her eyes all night) and then
I tipped upstairs to dress, past Milo and Macey who
were nodding stiff-necked in chairs, but when I came
down again, Mama was frying me some breakfast. I
wasn't hungry but I didn't mention it. It would have
just started Mama arguing and waked up Sledge. He
was sleeping sound when I left—the picture of Mildred, already the picture—and it wasn't till I left that
I knew how glad I was to leave and not have to sit
there all day, waiting for Sissie to go off like a dynamite
cap. Well I worked hard through the morning and
didn't get to call up home till lunch. Baby Sister answered and said there was no news yet and none in
sight so I didn't call again but waited till I could get
home and see for myself and when Mr. Coleman let*

*me out on the road at six, I could see there was some
sort of news to hear as every light in the house was
burning and every chimney smoking and Dr. Sledge's
car was there and when I got closer I could see the fire
from one cigarette on the porch. It was Milo standing
in the cold. I walked up to him and said, "What is the
news?" He said, "All I know is, it started at one o'clock
and hasn't got no better since." It is 9:20 p.m. as I
am writing this sentence and things have gotten worse
and worse with Sissie yelling closer and closer together
till now I don't know when she finds time to breathe.
It seems alot to ask her to bear, her being a raw nerve
all her life. And it isn't easy on any of us—not now it
isn't. Mama and Mary—at least they are upstairs with
the doctor working but Baby Sister and I are just
sitting here in the kitchen and have been since six.
Nobody wanted a mouthful to eat so I have been
writing on and on to you and Baby Sister has been
rocking Mildred's baby and singing him songs like he
was hers (I know she wishes he was and the way he
lets her handle him, maybe he wishes so too) and Milo
just penetrates back and forth through the house—and
out in the yard when the yelling gets extra bad. (He
has always said, nothing happens to people that they
haven't asked for. Well he asked for a boy but I don't
guess he bargained for so much noise.) Awhile ago he
asked me what would calm nerves. I told him a dose of
ammonia but he took camphor and got no relief and
has gone back out somewhere. I am wishing Macey was
here with him (he has gone to Raleigh for Mr. Isaac's
mystery-gift) because Milo is the one with the burden
now. Mama is pouring the ether to Sissie so fast she
doesn't know what is happening. I don't guess she does
though the way she sounds through plaster walls lets*

everybody know she is not having fun. Even Mildred's baby can hear her. He is tuning up to cry this minute, meaning hunger, so I will stop and fix his milk. Baby Sister drops him like a hot potato when he cries.

It is later now and right much has happened since I broke off. The main thing is, I was holding Sledge when Mama came down to find Milo. I hadn't seen Mama since breakfast but I knew the worst right away. I said he was outdoors so she stepped to the porch and called him. He must have come running because I could hear him panting in the hall. Mama told him, "It never even breathed" and he broke down. Then they went up to Sissie but I couldn't follow—mostly because I had Sledge still to feed. He seems to take to me now so I stuck with him. He is the picture of Mildred. But I told you that.

This means I won't be accepting your Thanksgiving invitation—not that I am needed here but I couldn't leave after this. Things will have to be quiet awhile.

Thank you Wesley, and excuse me now please,
Rosacoke

When the letter was done she felt she had stayed away long as she could, that her duty was to go upstairs and speak her regrets. She stood and smoothed her hair and rinsed her hands at the sink, but before she went she tipped to the stove to check on Sledge in his box. She reckoned he was asleep, having eaten just lately, but in case he wasn't she stopped where he wouldn't see her. And he wasn't. He was fumbling quietly with his dark hands at his eyes against the light. She stood a long time, watching, trying to picture his face as a boy's or a man's, but his features were closed on themselves like tight brown buds on a mystery-tree in spring. All she could see was Mildred that last cold day in the road, and it seemed to her she was more use here than upstairs talking to people that were each other's comfort so she took Sledge instead and sat back down and laid him in the groove of her lap, hoping she could make him smile one time and then go to sleep. She did a few quiet jokes with her face and hands to please him, but he only stared with his black eyes grave and his lips crouched cautious against her, and soon she gave up trying and commenced to sway her legs and hum low, and he twisted to the left and buried his face in her thigh and slid off to sleep. She waited. Then when it seemed safe she shifted one leg and rolled him back towards her, and he smiled at last as if in his sleep he saw better jokes than what she could offer. But that was all right. That was enough. And she sat still, hearing his steady sighing till she was nodding herself with her hands beneath his head.

Then Mary came to the door. "You done changed your mind about Sledge, ain't you, Miss Rosa?"

"No. He has changed his mind about me."

"Yes'm, he sure is. He don't let many hold him that way. He is a *shoulder* baby." She stepped towards Rosacoke and lowered her voice—"Well, give him here and you go on upstairs. I don't want him keeping you from your folks. Miss Sissie is sleep but Mr. Milo is setting by hisself in the front bedroom."

So Rosacoke passed Sledge to Mary and was almost at the door when the question came to her. "Mary, what is that baby's name?—Mildred's baby."

Mary looked to the box. "I expect it's Ransom,

Miss Rosa, but they ain't said nothing about *feeding* him."

Then Rosacoke went out and up the cold stairs, shivering. The door was shut where Sissie was, and she went on to the front room that was Papa's before he died. She knocked lightly there. Somebody made an answering sound and she opened on darkness. (Papa had never let them wire his room for light.) She said, "Who is in here?"

Milo said, "Me and this baby."

She had suspected that. She stood on in the door, seeing nothing, feeling nothing but the warmth of the room leaking past her, and finally she said, "Could I bring you a lamp or something?"

"No."

"Well, I'll be saying good night then, I guess." She stood a little longer, wondering what else she could say to a pitch-dark room. But he hadn't asked for anything else. He hadn't even said "Step in," and anyhow he was *Milo* and she hadn't been close to Milo for years, not since Sissie Abbott took hold and taught him whatever it was that changed him from a serious boy to the fool who sang her the Santa Claus jingle not two weeks ago. Then she closed the door and went to her own room across the hall. She took off her clothes in the dark and stretched out to rest. But she didn't sleep. She heard a man's footsteps leave Sissie's room and go downstairs and a car driving off. That would be Dr. Sledge. Then Mama came out and went to Milo and asked was he setting up all night? He said "Yes" and Mama said, "Son, I have got to rest. How come you don't go set in yonder with Sissie? I'll send Mary in here." Milo said, "Did Sissie tell you to ask me that?"

Mama said "Yes" and he said "Get Mary first" so Mama went down and sent Mary up, and then there was the sound of Milo walking past Rosacoke's door towards Sissie Abbott. When Rosacoke had heard that she said to herself, "They will all get over this soon. Wasn't that a child they never saw alive or called by name? It was God's own will and Christmas is coming. Just *sleep*." Then she slept.

Sunday afternoon when it was time, Mama and the preacher were upstairs with Sissie who was not resigned, and Milo was shut in Papa's room. He had been there since Mary left that morning. He had seen two people all day—Mama and Macey Gupton—and he had spoken twice. (When Mama took him breakfast he said, "Get Macey and ask him will he go to Warrenton for the casket." Macey did that and after dinner when Mama had ironed him a shirt and taken in his clothes and asked was he ready, he said "In a little.") But Rosacoke was ready. She had been ready since ten o'clock when Mama came to her in the kitchen and said, "You have got to go speak to Sissie" so she went and just by opening the door, shook Sissie out of sleep. Sissie said, "You woke me up." Rosacoke said, "I am sorry for that too," and Sissie cried, not hiding her face but staring at the ceiling. Rosacoke had seen Sissie do a number of things but not cry silent so she went to the steps and called Mama. Then she went to her room and dressed in what black she had and waited for three o'clock.

At three she stepped on the porch to make a last arrangement with Macey who stood in the yard. She walked to the steps and said, "Macey, will you carry the casket?" He said that would be an honor but was Milo ready? She said "I hope so" and Macey laid his hat on the steps and went towards the door but was stopped by the preacher coming out and Baby Sister and Milo and, behind them, Mama who would stay with Sissie. (None of Sissie's people knew. It was how she wanted it.) Milo had the casket in his arms. It looked about the size of a package you could mail.

Macey said, "Milo, let Macey tote that."

But Milo said, "Thank you, no. I will," and they went to the car. Milo and the preacher sat in back. Rosacoke and Baby Sister sat in front with Macey who would drive.

Macey said "Ready?"

Milo said "Yes" and they cranked up and rolled to the road and turned right. Just before the house passed out of sight, Rosacoke looked back, and Mama still stood in the door, her black dress against the black hall behind her, and her white arms bare, surely cold. Rosacoke turned to the road and knowing they would ride in silence, chose that sight of Mama to fill her mind through the slow half-mile to Mr. Isaac's when she looked again—at the day this time. She thought, "It is the kind of day nobody wanted"—still and gray and low but so clear the wrenched, bare cherries looked gouged on the pond with some hard point— and she wondered, "Does Mr. Isaac know of this?" But she didn't speak aloud—there was nothing he could do with the news—so they passed him too, and none of them looked at each other, and since the pines were next, Rosacoke didn't think again but watched the road. A wind began and kept up the rest of the way —nothing serious but strong enough to twist little cones of dust in gullies and when they could see Delight, to sway Landon Allgood, the one person waiting, black by the grave he had dug.

Nobody else came. Nobody else knew (except what Negroes passed on the road and stared), and there was nothing but a few words said at the grave. What could they say but his name (which was Horatio Mustian the third)? Then Milo and Macey did the lowering. Landon put on his cap and came forward to shovel, giving off sweet paregoric like his natural scent, and they all headed back for the car—the men and Baby Sister first and Rosacoke falling in last. But before she had gone ten feet, Landon said, "Miss Rosa" —she stopped and he took off his cap—"I am mighty sorry for you."

She studied him a moment, wondering what he thought he was burying. She pointed half behind her and said, "It was *Milo's* boy."

"Yes'm," Landon said and stepped back to his work, and she went on to the others and they went home. Nobody had cried and what Rosacoke had noticed most was the new red dirt Landon threw on her father to fill his sinking.

And nobody cried riding home or during the supper they ate without speaking or, after Milo went up to Sissie (to sleep on a cot by her bed), during the long evening in the front room with Mama writing Rato the news and Baby Sister acting her paper dolls through flesh-and-blood stories till finally they all turned in. So Monday, seeing no real job at home, Rosacoke went to work and sent Wesley her long letter by Special Delivery without even looking to know what it said, knowing she hadn't faced up to Wesley yet— what he had done and wanted to do—but having in the death for awhile one thing big enough to hold her mind off whatever troubles she had. And the death worked in her like a drug, not making her sad but numbing the day while she worked and the cold ride home that night.

She was late getting home Tuesday night. It had rained all morning and in the afternoon turned cold, and the roads froze too slick for speed. It was nearly six-thirty when she walked up the yard to the house, and Mama met her at the door, saying, "Where have you been? You are too late now and I wish you had never worked today. Milo has broke our hearts. Directly you left this morning he drove off. He didn't say a word about where, and he left me with every bit of Sissie to handle and me thinking all day long he had gone off somewhere drinking like your Daddy. Well, nobody here laid eyes on him till a hour ago when he come in so quiet I didn't hear him. I was cooking our supper but Baby Sister was in the front room yonder. She had come home from school and dragged out some naked baby doll and was mothering that—singing to it. He went in there and just set by the fire. In a little Baby Sister took it in her head to go upstairs and ask Sissie could she have a few clothes to dress up that naked doll. She didn't mean harm but Sissie started crying and called for me. I didn't hear her but Milo did and tore upstairs, and when he saw the trouble, he grabbed up all the baby clothes he could find and said he couldn't pass another night with them things here and was taking them to Mildred Sutton's baby. Sissie couldn't stop him so she hollered, 'Yes, take every *stitch*. They are no use to me no more. The woman you get to have your other babies can buy her own mess or let all ten run naked.' Well, I heard *that* and caught Milo at the door and told him them things was too little for Sledge but I couldn't stop him. He was gone. He is still gone and hasn't eat a mouthful this whole day, and I don't know is he drinking or not."

Rosacoke said, "Give me the flashlight and I will go find him."

"I can't let you go in the dark," Mama said. "I was just getting ready to call up Macey and ask him to go."

But Rosacoke said, "Don't call in the Guptons for any more Mustian business." So Mama gave her the flashlight, and she went out towards Mary's. It was colder already and the sky was clouded. What moon there would be hadn't risen, but as long as she walked through open fields, she could see without light, and when she came to the black pines, she tried to walk in darkness—she knew every inch of the way and she wasn't scared—but the path was loud with frozen leaves and a briar caught at her leg so she switched on the light and walked in its yellow circle till she came out at Mary's. The only light at Mary's was shining from the kitchen where an oil lamp burned. Rosacoke flashed her beam round the yard to check for the turkey that was roosting high. Then she went to the front and knocked.

Mary came with a lamp and said, "Miss Rosa, it's *you*" and stepped on the porch and shut the door. "Miss Rosa, he is here and I think he is better now, but when he come I didn't know *what* would happen. He must have crept in while I was back in the kitchen because when I heard a noise in the front room and went to the door to see, he was *there*, just standing over Mildred's baby, staring down wild at all them clothes he had thrown on the bed. Child, I thought he was crazy, and I didn't do nothing but tip on back to the kitchen and get me a knife. I flung open that kitchen door, and I said, 'Sweet Jesus, come in here and help me.' Then I went back to do my duty, but he had eased and looked like hisself and was setting down by that baby, and when I said 'Good evening,' he just said, 'Mary, please cook me some eggs.' I said, 'Yessir, Mr. Milo, and you come talk to me while I fix them,' and he is eating right now in the kitchen."

"Well, let me go see him."

"Yes'm, but Miss Rosa, is he *give* us all them clothes?"

"They are his to give."

"Yes'm," Mary said and led her in. The first thing the lamp struck was Sledge, lying back amongst his new clothes.

Rosacoke said, "Ain't it too cold for him, Mary?"

Mary said, "I reckon it is" but kept on towards the kitchen and opened the door. The warm air met them and Mary said, "Look, Mr. Milo, we got us some company."

Milo looked up and said "Yes" and ate another mouthful and then said "Sit down, Rosa" like the house was his.

Mary said, "Yes, Miss Rosa, let me cook your supper."

Rosacoke said no, she wouldn't eat, but she took the other chair at the table, facing Milo with only a lamp between them, and Mary left. Milo didn't speak again or look up—just ate—and Rosacoke was quiet too. But she watched him (what she could see in the warm lamplight—his forehead pale as hers though he spent every day in the weather and his eyes like hers but his hair the color that, now she noticed, was one more thing their father had left)—and with all his three days' misery, he seemed for the only time in years like the first Milo she had run after, hundreds of miles through Mr. Isaac's woods, laughing, before Sissie Abbott gave him secrets, before he got his driving license even, when his beard was just arriving and they would sleep together in the same big bed if company came and she would rest easy all night and wake before sunup and turn towards Milo beside her and wait till the first gray light carved out his face on the pillow and then woke up the birds that sang. Still, it *wasn't* that first Milo—not after these days—but something changed, and she didn't know to what nor what new secret he kept there in his misery. But she had sat long enough, and she thought she should speak. She said, "Milo, if you want me to—"

He broke her off—"I am not taking them clothes back."

"Milo," she said, "them clothes are yours to give, and I didn't walk all this way to get them back."

Milo looked up. He had finished eating. "Well, why *are* you here?"

"I just came to say that if you want me to—" But she stopped again and frowned at the opening door where Mary stood with Sledge in her arms, the image of Mildred and awake.

Mary didn't see the frown. "You all just go on talking," she said. "It's chilly in yonder so I'll feed him where it's warm if Mr. Milo don't mind."

Rosacoke looked to Milo, thinking this was more than he would bear. But Milo said "Go ahead" and watched Mary walk to the stove and begin heating milk.

Rosacoke thought, "He is better than I reckoned"

and stretched out her arms and said, "Mary, let me feed him. He has taken to me lately."

Mary said "All right" and came on to hand him over, but Milo shoved back his chair and stood and laid about a dollar on the table and said, "I got to go. Rosa, are you coming with me?"

Rosacoke put down her arms. "I'm coming," she said, still looking at Sledge and Mary and seeing why Milo had to leave. Then she stood too.

In the door Milo turned—"I'm much obliged, Mary. That money is for my supper."

Mary said, "You paid for them eggs many times with that stack of clothes but we thank you, sir" and Milo left.

Rosacoke said, "Excuse me rushing, Mary."

And Mary said, "Go where you are needed."

So Rosacoke followed Milo. He was walking slow and she caught him just in the pines and switched on her light to help him see, but he speeded up and walked six feet ahead till they came to the field of cotton stalks. From there they could see the house and the light where Sissie was. Milo stopped and turned on Rosacoke. She switched off her light, knowing he spoke best in the dark, and he said, "What were you trying to tell me?"

"—That I will lay out of work if you want company."

"That would be mighty nice," he said and took a few steps towards Sissie's light, but before she followed he stopped again and faced her. "Sissie's awake," he said.

She said "Yes" and caught her breath to say what she knew was her duty—to ease him and lead him home—but in what moon there was, he was still too nearly that first Milo so she waited.

He waited too but when he spoke he said, "Go in the house to Sissie and Mama and say Milo is out yonder but he ain't coming in unless they give their word not to speak about clothes or baby again."

She said she would—it was all she could say, all he asked for—and went to tell Mama and Sissie. Mama said, "This house is one-third his. Tell him to just come on and rest," and Sissie said, "Yes do, but the baby was one-half mine."

Rosacoke went back and signaled from the porch with her light. Milo came on and when he got to the steps, she said, "They say come in but Milo, the baby was one-half Sissie's."

"Making the other half Milo's," he said and stood in the dark, not climbing the steps. Then he said, "Did Sissie tell you to say that?"

"Yes."

"But you didn't have to, did you?"

She couldn't answer that and he walked by her up the steps and into the house. She went in a little later and heard him in Mama's room. He was meaning to sleep there without saying good night to Mama and Sissie upstairs. Rosacoke went to the door—he had shut the door—and said through it, "I'll see you in the morning, hear?"

In awhile he said "O. K."

She went up and stopped at Sissie's door and told them he was home safe and sleeping downstairs and that she wasn't working tomorrow. Then she went to her own dark room in hopes of sleep. But she lay in the cold awake, not feeling Sissie in the next room awake —seeing only Milo's face at Mary's and hearing him break down Saturday night in the hall. She heard him over and over—*Milo* who was asking only her to share his burden—and she pictured the baby (that she never saw alive or called by name) till the baby was almost hers. Then the burden bore down on her hot through the dark. She took it and cried and it smothered her to sleep.

She slept till somebody's hand woke her in the clear early morning. It was Mama bending over and whispering fast, "Get up. Milo is up already and wanting to go. He wouldn't eat with me and Baby Sister but said he would wait in the yard for you so come on and feed him." Rosacoke raised up and stared out the window. He was standing halfway to the road with his back to the house, but the day was so bright against him she could see his hands at his sides that opened and shut on themselves and, beyond him, one white sycamore straight as diving. She threw back the cover but Mama said, "Let me say one thing—Sissie don't know I am speaking to you and wouldn't want me to if she did, but I have sat by her three whole days, and I know how she feels." Rosacoke stared on at the yard. "He is your brother, I know—he is also *my* oldest boy —but that don't make him ours. He belongs to Sissie Abbott, like it or not, and what has he said to her since the funeral except 'Good night'?"

"What are you asking me?"

"I don't know what to ask you. If it was just me I wouldn't say nothing but, 'Ride with him to Atlanta, *Georgia* if he wants to, just don't let him take up drinking'—he is too close kin to his Daddy for that— but Rosa, there is Sissie lying yonder—" She whispered that but she pointed to the far wall.

Rosacoke looked to the wall with sudden fear as

if Sissie herself had broke through plaster and stood before them. She said, "Listen here, Mama. Milo is an adult man that is old enough to know his mind. He has called on me for help. He may *be* Sissie's but Sissie can't help him flat of her back, and anyhow I have known him a good deal longer than Sissie Abbott so what do you want me to do?—say 'No' when he needs company?"

Mama only said, "Go with him today if he wants to go but keep him off liquor, and if there comes a time—Rosa, *make* a time—say to him, 'Milo, Sissie needs you bad.' "

Rosacoke nodded to make Mama leave. Then she dressed and went down past Sissie's shut door. She called up the man she worked for and asked to have a few days off because of death. He of course said "Yes" but hoped she could come back soon. She said she would try but things were in right bad shape. That left her free for Milo to use however he needed so she went to the door and called his name. He turned where he was—just his face—and she waved him in, but he stood, his fingers still working at his sides. She waited in the cold and thought, "Mama and Sissie are upstairs listening, and now maybe he won't come after what I said last night." Then she went to the kitchen and began cooking on faith, and soon he was there, stopped in the door, looking to test her face. She knew and turned full to him—the way he looked had lasted the night—and said "Come in."

He came and sat quiet at the table while she cooked, and they ate in quiet till he said, "Did you sleep good?"

"It took awhile but yes, I managed all right."

"That's good"—he stood and went to the window

—"because I was thinking we could take us a trip today, it being so bright."

"Where to?"

"Well, if we went to Raleigh, we could get Mr. Isaac's Christmas candy."

Before she could answer, Mama's footsteps passed in the hall overhead so she said, "Don't you reckon we ought to stay closer-by than Raleigh?"

He turned to her. "Look—are you sticking with me or not?"

She looked and said "Yes."

"Let's go then."

She scraped their dishes and left them in the sink and said, "I'll get my coat."

"Where from?"

"My room."

"All right, but come straight back."

She went up and got it and came down quiet past Sissie's door. Milo was waiting in the hall, and they went towards the front together. But Rosacoke stopped in the door. "Don't you reckon we ought to say where we are going?"

"You ain't expecting no Registered Mail, are you?"

"No."

"Then let's go."

They went through the yard with their backs to the house, not speaking, and just at the car they heard a knock behind them. Milo didn't wait but Rosacoke turned to the house, knowing where to look, and there was Mama in the window of Papa's old room upstairs. She hadn't raised the glass to speak and she didn't knock twice, but her knuckle rested on the pane it had struck. Rosacoke thought of the dishes she had left and opened her mouth to explain, but Milo cranked up and when Mama saw the smoke of his exhaust, she nodded so Rosacoke just gave a little wave towards the house. Then she got in and they rolled down to the road and, still quiet, headed left for the paving and the store. Milo stopped at the store. There was nobody in sight but some trucks were already there. He said, "Step in please and get the mail." She went, seeing he didn't want to answer folks' questions, and the only letter was one that had just then come from Norfolk. She took it to the car, and Milo drove off while she read to herself,

November 18

Dear Rosa,

I just got home from work and found your letter lying on my floor with them Special Delivery stamps all over it. They really had me scared for a minute! But I have recovered and want to say I was mighty sorry to hear about Milo and Sissie's bad luck. I had been looking forward to seeing their baby at Christmas as Milo told me last summer it would come in time to be in the show at Delight and him and me counted on being Wise Men with Rato if he comes home. Maybe you will think it is a little funny that I am not sending Milo a sympathy card or anything and am just writing to you but you never said what you meant that night about Milo being mad at me so I don't know where I stand and sure don't know why he was mad unless he has X-ray vision through trees at night. Anyhow I have always thought a whole lot of Milo and his foolishness and I hope whatever he was holding against me has blown over and that you will pass my sympathy on to him and Sissie. Sissie must be extra-let-down, toting it through all that hot weather so tell her too I am sorry.

I am also sorry you won't be coming for Thanks-giving with me and my friends because I reckon what you need more than anything now is a little cheering up but I see what you mean about staying home awhile till the coast is clear. When it is though and you feel the need of a change, come on up here. Just give me fair warning! And speaking of the coast being clear— I hope you aren't having any more old or new worries about our deer hunt and that the coast is all clear there too. Is it? Time enough has passed so it ought to be. I am stopping now to get this on the train.

Good night Rosa from your friend,
Wesley

She folded it carefully and thinking she would never read it again, sealed the flap with what glue was left. Then she laid it in her lap with the writing down and looked at the flat road before them. She didn't know what she had read. Her mind was like a bowl brimmed with one numbing thing—Milo's burden he had asked her to share—and what Wesley said was oil on the surface of that, waiting. But looking ahead she could feel Milo throw curious looks towards her so to stave off questions, she faced the window at her right, and if it was the letter Milo wondered about, he took her meaning and drove on quietly till he had to speak —"Do you reckon Sissie meant what she said last night?"

"I wasn't there to hear her."

He waited almost a mile to answer. "She said I could get me somebody else to take my children from now-on-out. Reckon she meant that?"

"I can't speak for Sissie," she said, still turned to the window.

"Well, thank you ma'm for trying," he said, but he left her alone with her burden, whatever it was, while he went on, watching both sides of the road for anything cheerful to mention. It took awhile to find such a thing, but when he did he took the chance and pointed past Rosacoke's face to the window—"Have you eat any pecans this year?"

She said "No," not seeing.

"I thought you was a great nut collector." He slowed down a little.

"That was in olden times."

"Well, we can get us some right now." He stopped on the shoulder of the road and said "See yonder?"

She looked gradually, at nothing strange, at things she had passed every November of her life and not seen, things that had waited—the rusty bank thrown up by the road and gullied by rain and, beyond in the sun, a prostrate field where nothing stood straight, only corn with unused ears black from frost and stalks exhausted the color of broomstraw, beat to the ground as if boys had swarmed through with sickles, hacking, and farther back, one mule still where he stood except for his breath wreathing white on the bark of a tree that rose up over him straight and forked into limbs with nuts by the hundred and twitched on the sky like nerves because a boy stood in the fork in blue overalls and rocked. Then Wesley's meaning sunk through her mind like lead.

But before she could swallow her awful gorge and speak, Milo jerked at her arm and said, "Come help me shake down some pecans."

"Milo, we better go home."

"What's the trouble?"

"Nothing. You ought to be home with Sissie."

"Sissie don't want to see me now, and Rosa, you said you was sticking with me."

She turned from the window to her lap, but the letter was there so she faced Milo suddenly—that first Milo, not changed. "I ain't studying Sissie, Milo. Take me *home*." He didn't answer that and with nowhere else to hide her face, she turned to the window again and the boy rocking yonder in the tree, and Milo took her home round miles of deadly curves not slowing once, staring only forward in mystery and anger with not one word for Rosacoke who could feel Wesley's burden grow in her every inch of the way, nameless and blind.

At home Milo stopped sudden in the road, and the tan dust from his wheels rolled past them. Rosacoke sat for a moment, facing the house but not seeing where they were, and Milo didn't move to help her out. He sat with his feet nervous on the gas and his hand on the gear-shift and his eyes forward, and when he had waited sufficient, he said "You are home."

She looked and said "I am home" but not as if being home was a comfort. Then she opened her door and left him, and before she could get through the yard to the porch, he had turned and roared off the way they came. But she didn't see him go or hear his noise. She was listening to hear some sound inside her maybe, but all she could hear was her feet in the crust of the ground and—when she went in and climbed the steps easy, hoping to pass unnoticed—the thud of her heart in her ears like wet dirt slapped with a spade.

Mama stood ready at the top by Sissie's door. "Where is Milo?"

Rosacoke looked behind her and pointed with the letter in her hand as if he was there on the steps. "Gone to Raleigh—to get Mr. Isaac some candy."

"I thought you was riding with him."

"No'm, he just took me to the post office."

"You *said* you was riding with him, didn't you?"

"Mama, *Milo* is all right. Just let me go."

"Are you sick or something?"

"I'm not feeling *good*."

"Well, do you want a aspirin?"

"I don't want nothing but quiet, thank you, ma'm," and she went to her room and shut herself in and sat on the bed and not taking off her coat, said to herself, "I have asked time off for death so I can't work today. I have got to just sit here and think." But when she had closed her eyes, she was seized by a shaking that started at the back of her neck and flushed down through her. At first she thought, "I will build me a fire," but the shaking went on and she dug both hands in her thighs and clenched her jaws and thought, "The room is not this cold," but that didn't calm her so she slackened her jaws and gave in to it and it rattled her teeth and passed on off.

When she was steady again she opened her eyes on the mantel and the picture there of her father and not having thought, took paper and pencil and wrote,

Dear Wesley,

No it is not clear—the coast you are talking about —and if you are a human being you will come here now and do your duty.

But she couldn't say more than that. She couldn't even say that and be sure, not yet. So she waited, managing in desperation to sleep through most of the day—through Mama peeping in to check and Dr. Sledge's visit to Sissie and what little cooking was done, waking three or four times and lifting the shade to stare across the road at naked trees but forcing herself unconscious again till finally at night a car turned in and woke her and she watched Milo come through the dark with candy in his hand and heard him climb to Sissie and say good evening to Sissie and Mama and sit with them, not speaking, and then in a little heard Mama step out and shut their door and Sissie say something Rosacoke couldn't hear and Milo answer her low and them talk on like that till they faded out and Rosacoke thought, "I have failed Milo and drove him back on Sissie, and they have gone to sleep"—which was somewhere *she* didn't go that night again.

Or many other nights that came after, though she took any chance to tire herself—working through weekdays hard as she could (working Thanksgiving at her own request) and in evenings at home, washing clothes, for instance, that were clean already and ironing till everybody but Mama was asleep and she would appear in her nightgown to say "Rosacoke, that's enough," and Rosacoke would climb to lie-out one more night between cold sheets with nothing but black ceiling to look towards or if there was moon, its glare on the floor boards and the unlit tin stove and the mantel and with nothing to hear but, inside her chest like her own fierce pulse, the thoughts she could speak to nobody—not to Mama or Baby Sister or her own dark walls (for fear Sissie Abbott next door might know) or even by mail to Wesley until she was sure.

It was a month's time and a Sunday afternoon before she was sure. Milo had carried Mama and Baby Sister to Delight to make plans for the Christmas pageant, leaving only Sissie and Rosacoke at home. Rosacoke had kept up a fire in her room most of the day and stayed there, but about five o'clock she thought of Sissie downstairs alone and felt guilty and went down to her. Sissie was shut in the front room with the stove broiling high, and when Rosacoke came in she barely spoke, just went on flipping some magazine to the end. Rosacoke commenced reading too but in a little Sissie stood and went to the window and looked at the half-dark and said, "Isn't it time they was home?"

Rosacoke looked out. "I guess it is."

"Wonder what is holding them up?"

Rosacoke said "I can't imagine." (She knew very well but she wouldn't say.)

"Well, I bet they are trying to find a Mary since I backed out. Your Mama said she didn't see no way to keep from offering it to Willie Duke Aycock when she gets home from Norfolk—unless they call on Marise Gupton and she is pregnant again."

Just to speak, Rosacoke said, "*Willie* will be a sight."

But Sissie took it wrong and turned on her. "You didn't expect *me* to go through with it, did you?"

Rosacoke said "No'm, I didn't" and Sissie cried a little, quiet and turned to the window. She had cried a good deal that month, but Rosacoke still couldn't

watch her so she stepped to the hall and took a coat
and not saying where she was going, went out and
walked down the yard. By the time she reached the
road, she had forgot Sissie. She turned right and looking down and saying to herself, "Pretty soon I have
got to *think*," she walked on in dust till the dark was
broken by the silly hoot of guineas in trees which
meant she was at Mr. Isaac's.

She faced the house and the pecan grove, hoping
it would give her several minutes' thinking, and yes,
there was one light coming dim through curtains from
the downstairs parlor. She thought, "They are all in
there with the light," and she pictured them—Mr.
Isaac nodding already since Sammy had fed him, and
Miss Marina queer for the winter, tuned to whatever
station came strongest on the radio, and Sammy maybe
waiting for word to take Mr. Isaac in his arms and put
him to bed—and when she had finished with them,
she walked on another little way before the glow of
car lights showed beyond the bend in the road. That
would be Milo and Mama so she ran off the road
down a slope, and when the car had passed and dust
had sifted back over her, the guineas broke in again.
She looked towards their noise—she was almost at the
pond—and behind the pond in trees, she could just
make them out on the sky, huddled in black knots
from the cold. She wondered what was after them
before real night and for something to do, went on in
hopes of finding the trouble. She stopped at the pond.
She had not really seen it since summer drought—
not close—and she walked out on the short pier, her
feet on the boards sounding far. By what light was left
she could only see that the pond had filled its banks
with recent rain and swamped the rotten boat staked

by the pier and that it was gray, but the guineas kept up their noise, and Rosacoke said to herself, "It must be a hawk that is troubling them."

Then the weight of her own trouble spewed hot up through her chest and throat into her mouth. She gripped hard against it but it prized her teeth open and forced her to say out loud at last, "What am I going to do?" No answer came so she shut her eyes and, locked and blind, brought up in a rush, "Wesley Beavers tinkered with me six long years, wanting nothing but his pleasure, and when he finally took it dishonest and collected the sight of me in a broom-straw field, giving all I had, to mix in his mind with the sight of every cheap woman that has said 'Yes' to him, what did he hand me in return but this new burden that he knows nothing about? And if he turns up home for Christmas, won't he count on having me time and again, free as water? And if I was to tell him the trouble he has put me in, wouldn't he just sneak off to Norfolk by night and rejoin the Navy and sail for— Japan—and leave me not one soul to speak to and nothing to do but bow my head and sit home with Sissie Abbott staring and Mama maybe crying out of sight and Baby Sister playing her flesh-and-blood games and Milo joking to cheer me up while I wait for this child to take its time and come, bearing Wesley's face and ways but not his name?" Then she looked to the trees across the pond and took breath and said again, "What must I do?"

Like an answer, a piece of yellow light showed slowly in the trees near the ground, moving towards her. Against the black she couldn't see what made the light or was bringing it, but by its color and swing, she guessed it was a lantern, and nobody toting a lantern was up to mischief so she stood on and soon heard feet in the leaves. When the light had reached the far edge of the pond, whoever held it stopped for a little and then said gently across the water, "Who is that yonder on the pier?" It was Sammy Ransom's voice.

"Nobody but Rosacoke, Sammy."

"Good evening, Miss Rosa. I'll come speak to you."

He walked round the pond to where she waited and set his lantern on the pier. Its warm light struck along the barrel of the gun he held. "What you fishing for here so late?"

"Nothing much. I was just walking on the road and heard the guineas fussing and came down here to investigate."

"Yes ma'm. That's what I was just now doing myself. Miss Marina heard them in the house and sent me out here, saying it was a hawk."

"That's what I thought."

"No ma'm. Most hawks is sleep by now. I don't know what ails them fool guineas. Just old age, I reckon."

"How is Mr. Isaac, Sammy?"

"Not doing so good, Miss Rosa. Look like it's his mind now. He just rambles round inside hisself and don't know who me and Miss Marina *is* half the time."

"Do you reckon he can go to Delight next Sunday for the pageant?"

"Yes ma'm. If he live."

"Well, they are planning to give him a present."

"Yes ma'm. What sort of present?"

"A rolling chair, I believe."

"He don't need no rolling chair long as Sammy's around."

"I know that but Macey Gupton was the buyer."

"Yes ma'm. Well, we'll be there to get it if the Lord be willing." Then he thought to say, "Are you in the show this time, Miss Rosa?"

"No, not me."

"I remembers you from last year. Reckon will Mr. Wesley be in it again?"

"I don't know, Sammy. I don't even know if he is coming home."

"Don't you? Miss Rosa, I thought it was near-about time for you all to get married."

"No."

"Well, when is your plans for?"

"There are not any plans."

"Lord, Miss Rosa, I thought you had a *good* hold of him."

She waited in silence for the answer to give him, trusting it would come directly. But no answer came. She could not know yet how his one word *hold* had struck her mind dumb or what it would show her, in time. She could only say to herself, "I have known Sammy Ransom all my life—he has played baseball on our team—so I know he meant me no harm by that."

And to save her from speaking at all, a door slammed up at the house. They looked and there stood Miss Marina in the back-porch light, facing them. She could not see the lantern, but she beckoned now and then with her arm, and Sammy said, "Miss Rosa, I would ride you home, but you see they need me yonder." Rosacoke nodded and he took the lantern and said "Good night" and started for the house. She watched him go five yards, his right side in warm light and the shotgun dark on the left, and she thought for the first time in her life, "I cannot walk home in this dark" so she called out "Sammy—" not knowing what she would ask though for months she had had one thing to ask him.

He turned in his tracks. "Ma'm?"

But she asked what she needed most now. "I was wondering could you spare me that lantern just to get home with?"

"Oh yes'm. You take it."

She went on to him and took it and said, "I am much obliged to you" and headed for the road and home with the lantern in her clenched right hand, swinging close to her side, casting light upwards to her face sometimes and her eyes that didn't really see the road but were staring inward at what Sammy Ransom had showed her (not knowing what he did)—a Sunday evening in early November and her having been led on past a hawk by the curious sound to stop in trees at the edge of a clearing and look across a gap through falling night to Wesley Beavers, locked alone with his own wishes in the music he made on a harp with his mouth and moving hands that caused her to say to herself, "There ought to be some way you could hold him there" and then go forward to try a way.

At home she set the lantern on the porch and went by the kitchen where they all were eating to write this letter in her room—

December 15

Dear Wesley,

I guess you will be wondering when you see this

how come I have waited so long and am turning up now so close to Christmas. The reason is, you asked me something I didn't know a sure answer to but now I do. The coast or whatever you want to call it is not clear and I thought you better know that before your Christmas vacation begins in case you want to change your plans some way. (I haven't heard anybody speak of your plans for coming. You say other things in your letters but you don't say you will come.) I mean, maybe you won't want to come here now. Well what I want you to know is, I have thought this all out and I am not glad but I can't blame you if you don't show up, as it is me I hold responsible, and what I have done, I reckon I can live with. That is the news from

Rosacoke

—which she couldn't mail. She waited.

THREE

THE Sunday morning before Christmas (Christmas being Wednesday that year), Milo left Mama and Rosacoke cooking dinner and Sissie lying down upstairs and drove to Warrenton to meet Rato who had set out by bus from Fort Sill, Oklahoma two days previous and had ridden upright through four states, barely closing his eyes, to get home—not because after nine months away he wanted so much to see his people or to leave camp awhile and certainly not to be in a Baptist pageant but in order to pass out the gifts he had bought with his own money and to show the family in person his Expert Marksman badge and the uniform he meant to wear for the next thirty years if the U.S. Army would let him.

When Milo was gone Mama set Baby Sister as the lookout. She squatted at the dining-room window and stared to the road through the dull cold day till an hour had passed and dinner was ready on the stove. Then a car came in sight with two people in it and turned towards the house. Baby Sister hollered "Here is Rato!" and threw herself out the door to meet him. Mama left the kitchen just as fast, not putting on a coat, and they got to him halfway down the yard. He had never been much on kissing, but he let Mama touch him on the cheek and gave Baby Sister his free hand to pull towards the door where Rosacoke stood (the other hand held his duffle bag). When he was almost at her, he set down the bag and pulled his hand out of Baby

Sister's and stopped—not looking Rosacoke in the eye but grinning from under his overseas cap (the only clothes on him not wrinkled like paper from the ride).

Rosacoke didn't speak at first or smile. She was studying Rato with something like fear, and thinking back. He had come between her and Milo in age, and Mama had named him Horatio Junior for his father before she could see what was plain soon enough—that the mind he got would never make any sort of man. He had grown up mostly of his own accord, running sometimes with Milo and her and Negroes and taking what candy Mr. Isaac offered but seldom laughing and never being close to a soul or asking a favor. Still, he had *been* there all her life until last April. He had sat by her on cold school buses till he turned fourteen and stopped school completely and she met Wesley Beavers, and after that he had spent every Saturday night looking on from the porch at her and Wesley in the yard saying goodbye slowly. He had gone with her to the Raleigh hospital that week they sat with Papa before he died. And always, if he was nothing else, he had been one thing she could count on not to change, which was what she looked now to know—covering his face with her eyes (long yellow face rocked forward on his neck). But nine months of Army had taught him nothing new—thirty more years wouldn't either—and he had her father's name. So she held out her hand and smiled and said, "Merry Christmas, Rato. You have put on weight."

He said "Army food" and gave her his cool fingers to hold a little.

They all stepped into the hall and Rato stood again, not knowing where to set his bag. He never had a permanent room in the house but penetrated back and forth, stretching out wherever there was nobody else, and now Mama said, "Son, while me and Rosa's getting up dinner, you go to Papa's old room and put on your own clothes."

He looked at his wrinkles. "Thank you, no'm. These ain't mine but they are all I got."

Milo said, "What in the Hell you got that bag stuffed with then?—a woman?"

Baby Sister said, "Looks like Santa Claus to me."

Rato said, "That's what it is."

And Mama said, "Well, eat like you are but some of us will have to press that uniform before tonight," and she and Rosacoke went to lay out the food. Milo went upstairs to tell Sissie he was home, and Rato dropped his bag again and dangled in the hall with Baby Sister staring at him speechless. Mama called "Ready." Then Sissie crept down ahead of Milo. She spoke Rato's name and he spoke hers and said, "I have eat just peanuts since Friday" and stepped to the table before the others.

At the table Mama called on Rato for grace. There was considerable time while he searched for words, and Rosacoke thought, "That is mistake number one. After eight months away he's forgot," and Mama had opened her mouth to say it herself when Rato shot out, "Lord, I thank you for dinner."

They waited awhile for "Amen" but it never came so they looked up gradually and unfolded napkins and commenced passing bowls. They knew there was no point asking Rato about his trip or the Army—he had never made a satisfying answer in his life—but Mama couldn't pass up his grace without comment. "You all must not have much religious activities at camp, do you, son?"

Rato was red from his effort. He said "No'm," taking biscuits to butter.

And at first that seemed to stop other questions, but Milo thought and saw his chance—"What about them talks on women the chaplain gives?" Rato grinned at his plate and chewed and Milo kept on. "I certainly hope you have been attending *them*." Rato still didn't speak though Mama was watching him. Milo said "Have you, Rato?"

Sissie for a change raised eyebrows over the table to Rosacoke, meaning "*Brother* is closer kin than *husband*. *You* stop him," and Rosacoke said "All right, Milo."

Mama said "Yes, stop" but she was curious now, and when there had been quiet eating for a little, she said, "Are they some kind of marriage talks, son?"

"I don't know'm. I ain't heard one."

Milo said, "Well, you have missed a golden opportunity, I'm sure."

"I don't know," Mama said. "Some folks don't want to get married, do they, son?"

Rato nodded. "I'm one of *them*."

And Mama had to make a new start. "Son, do you all have a chaplain just for the Baptists or does everybody get the same one?"

"I ain't seen a Baptist since April. Just Catholics."

"Well, you will see some tonight."

"How come?"

"Because we are retiring Mr. Isaac from the Deacons tonight."

"Is he still alive?"

Milo said "Sort of."

Baby Sister said, "We are also having the pageant and you are in it."

"No I ain't." (Every year since he grew too big for a Shepherd, he had begun by refusing his part.)

Milo said, "Yes you are. Me and you's Wise Men."

Sissie said, "Who is the third?" and when Milo and Mama stared at her, she saw her mistake and bolted a mouthful of food for the first time that day.

But her question hung above them plain as the swinging light so Rosacoke laid her hands on the table. She pushed back her chair and stood and took the empty biscuit plate. Only Rato looked at her but she looked at Sissie and said, "The third one is Wesley if he comes in time." Then she went to the kitchen and stayed there longer than it generally takes for biscuits.

When she was gone Mama said soft to Milo "Is he come?"

"He's here. I seen him at the store just now when we passed."

"Well, I called up his mother yesterday to see was he coming for the pageant. She said she just didn't know his plans so I told her we would practice this afternoon and to tell Wesley if he come. Has Willie Duke come?"

"Oh yes. That scrap-iron fool flew her in last night."

Rato said, "Is *she* in the show?"

"Looks that way," Mama said but with Sissie there she didn't name Willie Duke's part.

Rato of course didn't know what they meant, talking low, but he had finished eating, and as Rosacoke stepped back through the door, he looked to her and said "When is Christmas?"

She smiled and said "Wednesday" and sat down.

"How come you ask?" Mama said.

But Rato was on his feet and out to the hall and

back with his duffle bag. He stooped to open it. "Because I have brought you all presents from the PX. Everything is real cheap there."

Mama said, "That's fine, son. But wait till Wednesday."

He just said "No'm" and brought out six boxes. They were all very much the same size and in white paper with no name tags, but Rato weighed each box in his hand, trying to know them by touch. Finally he passed one to Baby Sister, and while the others watched his sorting, she opened it. At first it seemed like a red plastic sack, but she found a valve and blew, and directly it was a toy elephant with black eyes that rolled behind celluloid. She thought to herself it was a very strange gift for a twelve-year-old, but all she said was "Thank you, Rato."

He said "That's O. K." and stayed on the floor, but everybody else turned to Baby Sister, stuck with her blown-up elephant, wondering where to set it. Mama laughed a little and the others followed, even Sissie, so Rato looked to see why. When he saw the toy he jumped to Baby Sister's chair and grabbed it from her. "This here ain't yours," he said. "It's a baby toy" and he put it to his burning face and bit off the valve with his teeth. The elephant shriveled to a sack again, and Rato stuffed it deep out of sight. Then he rocked on his heels and studied the five boxes left. "Listen," he said, "I bought this stuff way before Thanksgiving so I don't know what is what." That was as much as he had said at one time ever in his life, and he started refilling his bag. The others tried but they couldn't help staring at Sissie. Sissie for a change held up. But that was the end of eating. Mama stood and said, "That's all right, son. Take your time. Christmas will be here too soon as it is. You and Milo just go in the front room and set. By the time me and Rosa wash dishes, we will have to get on to Delight and practice."

Rato said "Who is *we?*"

"You all that's in the pageant and me that's managing it."

Rato said, "Are you in it, Rosa?"

"No. I had my chance last year, remember?"

He said "Yes" and dinner broke up. Sissie went back upstairs to continue resting. Milo and Rato went to the front room to wait for Mama—Baby Sister followed in case Milo told jokes—and Rosacoke and Mama washed dishes.

In the kitchen when the last dish was dried, Rosacoke hung two wet towels on a line by the window and stood, looking sideways to the empty road, her face the color of the day. Mama saw her and knew she had put off speaking long as she could, that she had to find a way now to offer blind help. But Rosa was Rosa (her strangest child). She would have to study out what to say so she wiped round the sink and washed her hands and slipped on the narrow gold ring she always removed before working. When that was done Rosacoke was still locked at the glass. Mama walked up behind and not touching her, said, "Rosa, you have barely laughed since summer ended. I don't know why exactly but even if you *are* my own flesh and blood, I ain't going to ask the trouble. I just want to say, if you got any business that needs telling—well, I am your Mama." She stopped to take breath but Rosacoke didn't turn. "And another thing, if there is some person in that pageant you don't want to see, just stay here tonight. I will understand." (She didn't understand. She hadn't guessed what the real burden was.)

Rosacoke stayed facing the road and Mama walked to the door to leave. At the door she tried again. "Did you hear me, Rosa?" Rosacoke nodded one time and Mama went out.

But all Rosacoke had heard was the last, which worked in her mind as she saw Milo lead the others to the car and drive off to Delight. After they vanished she said to herself, "Even if I do feel like crawling underground, I will not sit here tonight and moan with Sissie Abbott. Mr. Isaac may die any day. He has been good to us, and I mean to pay my respects with everybody else, including Wesley Beavers." She had halfway turned to get her church dress and iron it when she caught in the side of her eye a cloud of dust at the far curve of the road. She had to look. It was nothing but Macey Gupton's truck headed for the practice (he was Joseph and was hauling Mr. Isaac's gift-chair on the back, held down by his wormy daughters that were Angels), but when it was gone Rosacoke couldn't leave the window. She had to stand and take the sight of whatever cars passed by.

And the awful car she expected came soon enough —the Beavers' tan Pontiac moving fast as if it was late, twitching to dodge great rocks and with one person in it who suddenly knew where he was and slowed at the Mustian drive almost to a stop but not seeing any sign of life to call him in (*some* reason of his own), rolled on by scratching his wheels. Rosacoke pressed her face to the cold pane and watched to the end. Then she could think, "That is all the proof I need," and the thought, being what she had waited to know, came almost like relief. She had not seen a face or enough to swear who was driving but she knew. She also knew she could not attend any evening service—Mr. Isaac dying or not. But what she *could* do came to her next. "I will walk over now and take him his candy and tell Sammy I can't be there tonight."

She went to Mama's room and found the candy where Milo had left it. She wrapped it like Rato's things in tissue paper. Then she climbed the stairs to comb her hair and get her coat—she had dressed that morning for Rato's arrival. On the way down she stopped by Sissie's door and spoke through it. "Are you all right?" Sissie said she was. "Well, I am just going to step to Mr. Isaac's—hear?—and give him our candy." Sissie said not to mind her so Rosacoke went on.

She went the back way—off the road through a half-mile of bare woods. Near as they were, she didn't really know these woods (Milo had warned her long ago—to keep her from always trailing him—that somewhere in here was a place named Snake's Mouth where all snakes for miles got born, and the story had served his purpose till she was too old to explore), and looking down she walked through pine straw and waiting briars fast as she could, not because she was scared but because after watching the tan car fade, she didn't mean to stay in silence longer than she could help, even if Sammy Ransom was the only thing to talk to. Still, it took much longer than she hoped, and when she broke out of trees at last on the edge of the grove with the naked road on her left and Mr. Isaac's before her, she all but ran the hundred yards to the porch, and the pounding of her feet on dead earth flushed waves of screaming guineas into pecan limbs. The porch was not much help. The soft boards gave under her weight like carpet. The only thing moving was a dirty rocking chair, and the truck was nowhere in sight. She gripped the package and pulled with her chest for breath. Then she said, "Sweet Jesus, let *somebody* be here" and knocked.

And Sammy came, clean in blue work clothes, looking glad to see her. He stopped on the sill with the screen door between them. "How are you, Miss Rosa?"

She couldn't speak at first but she blinked her eyes and smiled. "Kicking, but not high, Sammy."

"You look a little pale, sure enough. I hope you improves by Christmas. Can I help you, please ma'm?"

She showed him the package in her hand. "Sammy, I won't be going to Delight this evening to honor Mr. Isaac with the rest. I got to stay home with Milo's Sissie so I brought him his candy. It's from all of us though."

"He be glad to see that, Miss Rosa. He and Miss Marina eat up all they had last Friday, and I ain't been able to leave him to get no more. But he don't understand that and yesterday evening after I got him in the bed, I left him for just ten minutes, and he worked hisself to the edge and commenced rummaging in his table drawer till he found one of them little cakes of hotel soap that he got twenty years ago—in Richmond, I reckon—and Miss Rosa, he *eat* about half of it before I come back and saw lather foaming round his mouth. (He is mixed up, you see—thinking about nothing but hisself all day.) But it didn't seem to hurt him none so I just wiped him off and didn't tell him no better. Yes ma'm, he be glad of this and so is Sammy." But he stood on in the door, blocking her way.

So she had to ask. "Well, if he is all right now, reckon could I speak to him a minute?"

Sammy smiled and lowered his voice and peeped behind him. "Yes ma'm. I was just holding off to let

Miss Marina hide. She don't see folks in the winter."
Then he stepped back and Rosacoke passed.

She had been in the house maybe forty-five minutes of her life, but she knew right away it was all the
same, the way it had been every Christmas-visit since
she could remember—the dark low hall, broad floor
boards stretching to the back (bare and polished from
the little walking since Miss Marina threw out the rugs,
saying "Moth hotels!"), green curtains drawn across
the four room doors (Miss Marina hiding back of one),
the rose love seat and the tired, preserving air that held
it all from one year to the next, unchanged and clean
and stifling as a July night. The one new thing was
hung by the parlor door—a calendar for the present
year (with a picture of a new Buick car and the sea
behind), turned to December with each day circled
through the twenty-first. Sammy saw Rosacoke notice
that—"Miss Marina is counting off the days to Christmas"—and led her to the far door on the left, saying,
"Stand here, please ma'm, while I get him fixed. I got
him in the bed, resting up for this evening."

She thought, "I have never been in this room. It
is the last place on earth Mr. Isaac in his right mind
would ask me," and she said, "Sammy, don't bother
him now. You give him this."

"Oh no'm. He be glad of company. It's the only
thing he glad of now. He might not know you though,"
and he went through the curtain, but Rosacoke could
hear every sound. Sammy said, "Set up, Mr. Isaac. I
got you a guest," and there was heaving of the bed as
he propped the old man on pillows. Mr. Isaac bore it
quiet as a sack of seed, but when Sammy had finished
and headed for the door to get Rosacoke, Mr. Isaac
tapped on wood and Sammy went back. Rosacoke

could hear him hawking at his throat and finally his whisper, "Brush my hair" so Sammy poured water to damp his head and brushed him and said "Now you ready" and called Rosacoke.

She stepped through and saw first thing on the opposite wall three pictures of people—the only one she knew being Franklin D. Roosevelt, torn off *Life* magazine, tacked up, crisp and curled and happy, over a bureau that lacked a mirror and had nothing on it but dust from the road and a tortoise-shell hairbrush. The rest of the room was just that bare—her eyes passed over a low washstand with a pitcher and bowl and the black leather chair and one wide window and a long rusty wall till she found Mr. Isaac in bed way round on her left, too far to see his pictures. She went three steps towards him, and Sammy said, "This is your friend Rosacoke, Mr. Isaac."

She was not his friend. She had never been more to him than one of Emma Mustian's dusty children in the road—the one that had grown up bringing him every Christmas the horehound candy her Mama bought to offer in partial thanks for the fifty dollars he gave when the children's Daddy was killed—but facing him now she knew she was right to come. He filled her mind already with something but bitter dread—set up on white pillows in a white flannel nightshirt with spotted hands flat on white sheets and still, for all Sammy's pains, looking dirty because his face had yellowed too deep to fade now and the hair above was streaked like old piano keys.

She went the rest of the way and held out the package. He looked at her offering hand and at her— the dead smile on the right side of his face but both sides blank as paper—and to Sammy beside her. Sammy said, "Take your present and thank Miss Rosa." He turned to his own hands before him and stared as though he would move them invisibly, by sight. Then his live hand commenced a flutter on the sheet like a learning bird in hopes of flight and reached out slowly to Rosacoke.

When his fingers had the package, she said, "Merry Christmas, Mr. Isaac. I hope you have many more."

But he didn't speak and his face didn't show even recognition. He carried his hand back halfway and held it at seeing distance, studying what he had. Sammy spoke though—"You want me to open it for you?"— and before Mr. Isaac could nod, took it and tore off the paper. "Look here, Mr. Isaac, you got you some horehound again. Ain't you glad?" The old man looked at the candy and then to Rosacoke for a long try at remembering, but if he knew her or why she had brought him this or was thankful, he gave no sign. Sammy said, "I told you, Miss Rosa" and broke the bag and laid two sticks of candy in Mr. Isaac's hand. The hand shut on them like a trap. Sammy said, "Miss Rosa, take a chair" and fetched her one with a horsehair bottom and set it near the bed.

She had no reason to stay (no reason she could mention), but what else could she do?—walk back through those woods again? or up the road where whoever passed could see her alone? and pull herself upstairs and feed her stove and sit on the bed with Sissie sealed in next door, needing comfort? and feel, one mile down the road, everybody she knew at Delight (Milo and Wesley and Macey quizzing Rato about women and joking with Landon Allgood—drunk but trying to sweep—and Baby Sister bossing Guptons and Mama pleading every two minutes, "You all *please* behave")? So she said, "Well, I *will* stay awhile" and pulled back the chair and sat and turned to Sammy, hoping he would talk.

He said, "You say you got to set with Miss Sissie this evening—how is she, Miss Rosa?"

"Dr. Sledge says she is all right—her *body*. It will take her some time yet to stop grieving though."

"Yes ma'm. It was a boy, won't it?"

"Yes."

"What was his name?"

"Rato."

"Named after Mr. Rato?"

"Rato was our Daddy's name."

"Yes ma'm."

Rosacoke turned to Mr. Isaac then, thinking he might help her change the subject, but he was only watching his shut hand and Sammy began again. "Well, I hope she gets her a new one soon."

"Sissie you mean?" but she didn't face Sammy.

"Yes ma'm."

"I don't know if she could stand it again."

"Yes ma'm. Don't look like folks been having much luck this year, does it?—Mildred Sutton, she died, and now Miss Sissie's boy." He waited but Rosacoke still didn't turn. "Is you seen Mildred's baby, Miss Rosa?"

"Yes."

"Don't he take after Mildred? I seen him last week. Estelle had him at Mount Moriah, and I seen him just from a distance. First time."

Rosacoke had looked for comfort from Sammy, but with what he said her heart was wild again, and she had tensed her legs to stand and leave when Mr.

Isaac came to life. He turned far as he could and tried to whisper to Sammy, "Who is her Mama?"

Sammy said, "Miss Emma Mustian. This is Rosacoke." And Mr. Isaac nodded. He didn't look at her or smile, just opened his hand and carried one stick of candy to his mouth.

Rosacoke had stayed to see that, and once it was done Sammy said, "Will you set here, Miss Rosa, while I go fix his medicine?"

She could only say "Yes" and Sammy went. Mr. Isaac watched him go and as his steps died out towards the kitchen, stared at the curtain, wondering maybe was that the last of Sammy. Rosacoke wanted to set him at ease, but he didn't look at her. He went back to his hand and took the next stick of candy and crammed the room with the noise of eating as if he was grinding teeth to powder. Rosacoke had to stop him. She said, "Mr. Isaac, I hear you are going to church this evening." But he didn't stop. He chewed to the end and swallowed, and she thought he hadn't heard. Then he turned on her—his eyes—and he started, "I—I can't die. If you was to shoot me, I wouldn't die. So I don't pray." He pointed to a spot on the bare floor between them —"I—I—I don't pray no more than that dog does yonder."

There was not any dog. There hadn't been a dog for fifteen years. There was only—out the wide window —high black trees stuck up on the far edge of the pond where woods began (where the deer was and the spring and the broomstraw field) and nearer, crawling cherries and water, hard on the surface but swarmed with cold slow-blooded fish, locking the rotten boat by the rotting pier, and there was no sound of Sammy coming so

Rosacoke got to her feet and walked to the wall and the pictures. She had saved them to look at if she needed—the ones she had not recognized, tintypes in round walnut frames on each side of Roosevelt, a lady about her age and a man about fifty. At first sight she knew the lady. It was Mr. Isaac's mother (Miss Marina, even crazy, was her image), and the man was his father —stern and bald, screwed to the chair he sat in, one empty sleeve pinned up at his shoulder. He had given an arm in the War. (Mr. Isaac had told her years ago when he met her one day in the road and asked for the hundredth time who was her Mama. She had said "Emma Mustian" and then asked who was his Daddy. He had told her, "Dead—died at ninety and his last words were, 'I do not understand.' But Cas was his name. He fought at Vicksburg and lost his arm and didn't eat nothing for forty days till him and his men caught rats." She had said, "No wonder he died" and had gone on home, Mr. Isaac laughing behind her.) Recollecting that was a help and she turned to the bed. "Mr. Isaac, is this your Daddy here?"

His hand was on his yellow hair—just smoothing— and he kept that up as he strained his eyes to the wall and said, "Papa told me I would be bald as him but I ain't."

That helped a little too. (He was right. He had never lost a strand—except what was in his brush—and the sight of it now brought her the memory of when Milo was ten and came in one morning from the store with what Mama sent for, plus a nickel. Mama asked where he got it, and he said, "I was coming out the store, and Mr. Isaac was setting on the steps in the shade, and he said to me, 'Boy, I will give you a nickel to scratch my head.'") And when that had run through her mind like spring water, she felt she could sit again for as long as Sammy was gone and she was needed. She went to the chair, stepping careful not to jar what little calm she had made, and when she sat, knocking came from the front of the house. At first she wondered was it Miss Marina and had Sammy heard. But his footsteps passed from the kitchen to the front and opened the door. For all the quiet she still couldn't hear who was there or what Sammy mumbled till he spoke up at last—"Step on in. She's watching Mr. Isaac for me"— and led somebody towards her. She didn't face the door or stand. She faced Mr. Isaac and when Sammy drew back the curtain, cold air struck her neck and Wesley spoke her name. Her legs thrust up and twisted her round to see where he stood, his face like a weapon against her.

With the breath she had she said, "Why have you trailed me here?"

Sammy brought him on by the arm, and Rosacoke backed till the bed stopped her. Nothing was between them but the dead air her chest refused. Wesley said, "Your Mama sent me home to get you, and Sissie said you was here. You see, Willie Duke has eloped by air with Heywood Betts to Daytona Beach, and you got to be in the show tonight so come on with me to practice." He smiled and Sammy Ransom smiled behind him.

Rosacoke would have run—she had already whimpered, cornered and wild, in the roof of her mouth— but something touched her coat from behind, and she flung backwards to see what it was. It was Mr. Isaac. He had slid to the edge and reached for the candy and knocked the broken bag against her back with his liverish hand and was smiling on both sides of his face, his old teeth parted, the stink of his age leaking through them. There was nowhere better to turn so Rosacoke stared on and shuddered. Then he lifted the candy towards her and whispered, "Give this to the children."

She frowned hard and Sammy came forward— "What children, Mr. Isaac? This is *your* Christmas present"—and took the candy from him.

But Mr. Isaac pointed to Rosacoke, "That is for the *children*," and Rosacoke ran past Sammy and Wesley with their grins, through the curtain, past Miss Marina hiding, to the door and the porch, towards the road, headed God-knew-where, but away from Wesley Beavers who didn't *know* and who wouldn't care— hair and coat like old flags behind, legs pumping noise from her belly through her nose to drown his nearing steps (low sick whines like nothing she had made in her life, that her teeth couldn't stanch).

Her breath lasted halfway to the road, and terror took her another few yards before Wesley came close enough to touch her shoulder lightly. That touch— asking, not clutching—sent tiredness through her like a killing shock. She ran beyond his hand. Then she stopped. He was somewhere behind her. She didn't know how far. She didn't care. She just had to rest. Her head slumped towards the ground as if she would never look up, and hair fell over her face. Then he touched her again. She was too numb to feel anything but weight so his right hand stayed on her shoulder as he came round in front and rocked her chin towards him. (He had never done such a thing in daylight before.) Her skin was paler than usual, and her eyes wouldn't meet him though they were dry as sand. But those were the only signs—why should he understand those? He said, "Sweet Jesus, what ails you, Rosa?"

She drew her chin back towards the ground. "Nothing you can cure." Her voice was like a croupy child's.

"Tell me what's your trouble."

"If you don't know by now—"

"I don't know nothing except you are acting mighty strange for Christmas." He slid his hand down her arm and took her cold fingers—she let them go like something not hers—and said, "Come on now, Rosa. We got to go practice. Everybody is waiting. We'll have a *good* time."

She shook her head, meaning No, and shut her eyes.

"Rosa, Willie Duke has eloped and you got to take her part, else your Mama's show will fold up."

Her eyes stayed shut. "Marise can do it."

He laughed. "Then you ain't seen Marise lately."

She shook her head again but her eyes opened.

"Marise can't be in no Christmas show *this* year. She is swole-up with baby-number-five the size of that house yonder." He pointed to Mr. Isaac's and Rosacoke turned her head to see. Sammy Ransom stood on the porch. He had run that far with Wesley and waited to know if he was needed. Wesley hollered, "It's all right, Sammy." Sammy smiled and waved and went in.

Rosacoke said "No it ain't," not meaning to speak, feeling it slip up her throat.

"What ain't?" Wesley said and reached to take her other hand.

But she stepped back. Her hands twitched a time or two, and to calm them she smoothed one side of her hair. Then both arms went straight at her sides and the fingers clenched. "Marise Gupton ain't the only one working on a baby." Her voice was almost natural, just tired.

"Who are you speaking of?"

"I am speaking of me."

He didn't come to her so they stood a long minute like that, stiller than they had ever been, four feet of day between them. Wesley was downhill from her and lower, facing the yellow house (the pecans, the guineas, Miss Marina peeping) but seeing only Rosacoke in his head—the way she had looked that November evening by flashlight in broomstraw, the way she looked now, almost the same, just tireder. But Rosacoke stared past his head (his hair grown dark and long for winter) and stopped her eyes on the road that was empty. She said one thought to herself as a test—"Wonder have many other women told him this?"—and she waited for the hurt but it didn't come. Her mind was empty as the road. She was numb to Wesley Beavers for the first time in eight years, numb as a sleeping leg.

But Wesley was not, not now if he had ever been. He said slow and careful, "Understand what I say— you don't know nobody but me, do you, Rosa?"

She said "No," not looking.

He took a long deep breath and let it out. "Well, come on then. We got to go practice." His car was up by the house, and he wandered towards it, not taking her hand as he went. He had to think and he was trying, the only way he knew—by draining his eyes and his mind of everything and waiting till an answer rose to the surface. He had gone ten yards before he knew he was walking alone so he stopped and twisted one foot in dirt. Rosacoke heard that and turned her head a little. He said "Rosa?" and started again for the car. And she came on behind. It would be somewhere to rest.

* * *

They rode without speaking, separate. Wesley's hands hung from the top of the wheel, and his forehead leaned almost to the glass—his eyes flat and blind—not to see Rosacoke till he knew how to speak whatever he decided. Rosacoke's hands were palm-up, dead, on knees that had gapped apart to let her eyes bore through to the floor. So both of them failed to notice the one thing that might have helped—rare as lightning in late December, a high white heron in the pond shallows, down for the night on its late way south, neck for a moment curved lovely as an axe handle to follow their passing, then thrust in water for the food it had lacked since morning. But in no time the church had swung into view and still Wesley didn't know. He glanced at Rosacoke—she hadn't seen where they were—and drove on a ways with the woods around them, to wait for what he must do and the words to speak it in.

Then the words came to him, and he pulled off the road. Rosacoke thought she was there and reached for the door handle, but he had stopped by the tracks that led to Mr. Isaac's spring. Far as she could see, only briars and frozen weeds stretched into thickening pines, and Wesley's eyes were pressed against her face, waiting for something from her. He said, "Rosa, how come you ain't told me sooner?" His voice was almost happy. It was the beginning of his offer.

But she said, "Take me to Delight please."

"We got to talk some, Rosa."

She said, "I don't owe you two words," but still he looked and gave no signs of moving. So she made one try to save herself the walk—"Am I riding to Delight or have I got to go by foot?"

He would have to finish what he had begun, but

he saw she could not listen now. He knew she was tired and that seemed reason enough. Anyhow, he had never begged anybody for anything, and he didn't know how to start at age twenty-two. He said, "You are on your way" and faced the rear window and turned in Mr. Isaac's old tracks and drove her back slowly, guessing she only needed time to calm herself and listen. He stopped fifty yards from the church by Milo's car near the graves. Rosacoke looked up again—at creek sand now, like snow, and the square white building—and she thought, "How in the world can I troop in yonder, smiling, and practice this part for tonight, knowing all I know?"

In her wait Wesley reckoned he saw another chance. He said, "Rosa, why ain't you told me before now?"

She faced her window. "What good would that have done?"

"It would have saved wear and tear on your nerves. You look right peaked." He sounded as if he was smiling—"And if I had had warning, I could have spoke to Heywood Betts, and we could have flew off with him and Willie to Daytona Beach for Christmas!"

She said, "I have not been sleeping much. Don't joke with me."

He said "I ain't" and when she moved to get out, he laid a hand on her wrist and looked to the church to see was anybody watching. "Listen here. We will drive to South Carolina tonight when the show is over. To Dillon. That's where everybody goes—you ain't got to wait for a license there. Then we can head on to Myrtle Beach if it ain't too cold and collect a few shells and get back here on Christmas Eve. O. K.?"

She left his hand in place, thinking it meant nothing now, but she said, "I am not *everybody*. I am just the cause of this baby. It is mine and I am having it on my own."

"Not a *hundred* per cent yours, it ain't. Not if what you say about knowing nobody but me is *so*."

"It's so."

"Then we got to go to Dillon this evening." It was that simple to him.

She shook her head and gave him the first reason that came—"It would break Mama's heart."

"It'll break a heap louder if her first live grand-baby comes here lacking a name."

"Hers ain't all that will break."

"No, I reckon not. I ain't exactly glad it happened this way myself, but it don't upset my plans too much. I mean, I have paid up my debts. Every penny I make from here on out is mine. We can live. Anyhow, we done this together and—"

She knew she could not bear the end of that, whatever it would be. They hadn't done *nothing* to-gether. She stepped to the ground and went on towards the church. Wesley watched her go three yards. Then he got out himself, intending to catch up beside her, but the sound of him coming quickened her walk so he followed at the distance she chose—not understanding, hoping he just had to wait.

And she would have gone in ahead as she meant to if halfway across the grove, she hadn't heard the choir door open, rusty, at the side and seen Landon Allgood tip down the steps and head across her path, weaving enough to show his condition and dressed for summer but with both arms full of holly—thorned leaves and berries that shined at her clean through the grove like cardinals hunched against Landon from the weather. She wondered, "What does he need with holly like that?" (It was plain he was taking off some of Mama's best decorations. Greens like that only grew deep in Mr. Isaac's woods, and the youngest boys had spent all yesterday gathering them.) But she had no idea of asking, and she stepped along faster not to meet him. He hadn't noticed her and she thought she was safe till Wesley called out from behind, "You look like a holly bush, Landon," and Landon stopped to lift his cap but seeing his arms were loaded, smiled and came on. Rosacoke told herself, "There is no way not to speak now—him this near and Christmas on Wednesday" so she stopped too, and Wesley reached her the same time as Landon. She said "Good afternoon, Landon," trying just to answer his grin and overlook the holly.

But Wesley said, "Where are you taking all them greens?" He was grinning like Landon. He took this meeting as a sign.

"They is just some little Christmas greens for Mary, Mr. Wesley." (Mary Sutton was his sister.) "She say she would give me my dinner if I find her some Christmas greens."

"Well, you sure found some grand ones, didn't you?"

"Yes sir, I did. I don't know who she decorating for except that baby, and it don't know holly from horses' harness."

"I don't reckon so. How old is it, Landon?" He didn't need to know. It was just the next thing to say.

"I don't know, sir. It won't walking last Tuesday though."

Rosacoke had to speak. "His name is Sledge and he come in late July."

"Was it that long ago?" Wesley said, glad she had offered *something*, and she nodded, looking off.

Landon said, "What you asking me, Mr. Wesley?" He had not kept up.

But to stop Wesley's answer Rosacoke said, "I got to go practice, Landon. Let me just give you this." She felt for her purse but it was at home.

Wesley said, "What you hunting, Rosa?"

She didn't say, so Landon told him. "Sometimes she give me a dollar for my medicine I needs."

"—But I haven't got it now," she said. "I am sorry. Come by the house on Wednesday."

That was all right with Landon, but Wesley said "Here's your dollar" and reached for his money.

Rosacoke said, "*I'll* give it to him Wednesday."

"You maybe won't be here Wednesday."

"Where am I going," she said.

He smiled, not seeing she had not asked a question, and Landon looked back and forth between them, confused. But Wesley had already pulled out two old dollars. He stuffed them in Landon's pocket. "That'll cure a heap of toothaches," he said.

"Many-a-one," Landon said, bowing deep on his holly. "Thank you, sir. Thank you, Miss Rosa." Then as if it was his gift for them, he nodded to the side. Rosacoke knew where to look. "I been spreading new dirt on Mr. Rato where he sinking."

And there through the grove was her father under raw new dirt, changed to dirt himself after thirteen years, who had changed one time before—from the boy her Mama recollected, in white knee-stockings so solemn on a pier at Ocean View, to the drunk who killed himself one Saturday evening by mistake (like everything else he did) and left behind a tan photograph and four blood children (Milo with his hair, and Rato Junior with his silly name but no mind, and her with one or two awful memories, and Baby Sister working in Mama when he died)—and was sinking now by his Papa and Mama and his first grand-baby that would also have had his name if it had breathed, and someday might have passed it on. She said "Thank you, Landon" and in the church the piano started (that hadn't been tuned in memory), seeping through the walls as if from underwater, too faint to call a tune.

Landon said, "I wish you all a happy Christmas and many more to come" and started for the road and Mary's, and Rosacoke started for the church. But Wesley held her—his hand on her shoulder, not so gentle now. "You know I am serious, don't you?" She didn't pull away but she made no sign and she didn't look. "Well, I am. And you got all evening to think it over. Tell me tonight." He lifted his hand and she walked on but he didn't follow. He stood where she left him, waiting to know would she look back one time at least, wondering what had turned her against him, yet seeing how little her picture had changed since summer—her high legs lifting her on over sand like snow crust, working from her hips like stainless rods, steady and lovely (even now, toting their new burden) as if she was walking towards a prize.

She got to the steps and climbed and at the top, in the door, turned and not knowing why, not thinking, looked back the way she had come—to the car and the graves and her sorry father, then a little careful, still testing, to Wesley Beavers for the first time since Mr. Isaac's, looking down on him and thinking, the moment she met his eyes, "I am free"—a way she had seldom felt since the November day eight years ago when he rained down pecans at her request, the way she had felt for maybe ten minutes that other November evening when she struck out for Mary's—after the hawk passed over and the music—as if her life was hers, till the wind turned and the music came back and pulled her through briars and roots to the Beavers' clearing where she could see Wesley on the porch, leaning on a post over his brother, his hair still light from the beach, his white sleeves rolled above dark hands that shaped the music, and his face not smiling no more than the hawk—sealed off with his private pictures, not seeing her, needing nothing he didn't have, but happy. Now everything was different. The distance between them—the space—was half what it was that evening. Now Wesley was flat on his feet with his arms pinned to his sides. His wrists had faded white and showed from the sleeves of his sailor jacket (he had grown some in the Navy), and his face was offered up towards her like a plate—with nothing on it she wanted, not any more. She told herself, "Well, I held him. I tried and I held him. I caused him this bad afternoon, and maybe I have ruined his Christmas and I am sorry. But I reckon he has learned one thing he never would have guessed on his own—that it is very lonely, donatings things to people that they don't need or even want—and he will be all right in awhile. He has paid up his debts. He can live. He hasn't got to take no share of this load I brought on myself. I am free from him. God knows I am free." She thought it was her right to think that, and if he had come on then when a final No seemed simple as breathing, she would have said it and saved him waiting till night. But the piano, that had strummed on alone under what she thought, crept into the first of a tune, and all at once there was a girl's voice, riding out pure as spring water. Rosacoke knew it and went in towards it, and Wesley followed in a little. It was Baby Sister. She was practicing "Joy to the World."

And she sang it that evening after they retired Mr. Isaac and gave him his chair and Sammy wiped his eyes and set him in it by the Amen Corner and Mama at the back switched off the lights and the pageant members took their stations unseen and most of the coughing calmed into waiting breath and the preacher recited in the dark, "And there were in the same country Shepherds abiding in the field, keeping watch over their flock by night. And lo, the Angel of the Lord came upon them, and the glory of the Lord shone round about them and they were sore afraid. And the Angel said unto them, 'Fear not, for behold, I bring you good tidings of great joy which shall be to all people.' "

She started it back in the Sunday school rooms out of sight, and the first words didn't carry, but she came on closer till soon every sound was cutting the pitch-black air like a new plow point, reaching some eighty people. Then she moved into sight—to join her song —through a door up front at the side, trailing behind her a swarm of humming girls, mostly Guptons, in cheesecloth veils with trembling candles that were all the light in the church. They were meant to be Messenger Angels, and Baby Sister's song was meant for the Shepherds, and when she was at the pulpit and the girls closed in around her, there they were—Moulton Ayscue and John Arthur Bobbitt and Bracey Overby, stretched on the floor in flannel bathrobes with peeled sticks beside them. At the touch of light they sprang up

afraid and crouched with quivering arms while she finished—

> *Let every heart*
> *Prepare him room*
> *And heaven and nature sing.*

Then the preacher went on. "And it came to pass as
the Angels were gone away from them into heaven, the
Shepherds said one to another"—and Bracey said, "Let
us now go even unto Bethlehem and see this thing
which is come to pass, which the Lord hath made
known unto us."

But Baby Sister's girls were the light. They
couldn't go away so they led the Shepherds slowly to
the choir where Macey Gupton stood as Joseph and
Rosacoke sat as Mary and Frederick Gupton, eight
months old, rested in a basket set on legs, as Baby
Jesus. The Shepherds stopped in front of him, and
Mama at the back switched on the overhead star and
the Angels circled behind. When the flames had
steadied in their hands, a ring of light crept past Rosacoke and Frederick till it reached the two front pews
and the Amen Corner where Mr. Isaac was. The Shepherds knelt in the center of that ring. Each one laid a
hand on the manger that rocked with the weight, and
John Arthur Bobbitt commenced to nod his head. On
his third nod the Shepherds sang ragged and thin,

> *Away in a manger,*
> *No crib for a bed,*
> *The little Lord Jesus*
> *Laid down His sweet head.*

They had been warned at practice to sing low enough
and not scare the baby, and the way they started there

seemed no danger, but still Rosacoke leaned over to see how he was. His head was turned away and a fist was against his ear—that was all she could see—but he seemed asleep, seemed safe, so she looked beyond the boys and followed the weakening light to its edge, and there was Mr. Isaac, ten yards away, dim. (Sammy was somewhere dark beside him.)

He had had a long full day—a full week, eating that cake of soap—and even in the dimness she could see his face was not calm yet. His face was *all* she could see, and silver spokes in the wheels of his chair, but she looked on awhile till she reckoned she saw other things, things she needed to see just then—that his eyes were set towards her, looking a way she had not seen before, not the blank look of his strokes or the old shielded way but unsatisfied, wondering, as if he might turn any minute and jerk Sammy's sleeve and try to whisper, "I do not understand" and point at her. She said to herself, "I ought to beg his pardon—acting so wild this afternoon, confusing him like this. What I will do is, go back to see him Christmas day if it's fair and tell him, 'Mr. Isaac, I have come to beg your pardon for my actions last Sunday. You have always been good to us, and I've felt mighty bad, running out on you like that, so I know you will understand when I say I am not myself these days. I am toting more load than is easy alone, if you know what I mean.' " She kept on staring and she wondered, "What will he say to that? When my Daddy was killed he drove to the house after dark and sent in for Mama and waited on the porch till she came and gave her fifty dollars, saying, 'Emma, he is far better off.' "

He waited through her thinking, still as he was that time they found his spring and him cooling in it

—her and Milo and Rato and Mildred Sutton. The candlelight trembled on his face—the Guptons were fidgeting—but she knew his look hadn't changed, that he did not understand, and looking inward till she couldn't see him at all, she told herself, "I can't just beg his pardon and not say *why* I acted wild. So what on earth can I do?—stand by his stale bed and point out his side window past the pond and say loud enough for him to hear (and Miss Marina up the hall), 'What I mean, Mr. Isaac is, one evening early last month I followed some deer in your woods. I thought they were headed for the spring but they weren't, and then I came to a broomstraw field you may not have seen and laid down under a boy I know that was with me. I have known him quite awhile—eight years last month. (I met him when we was just children in your woods, where there's a pecan tree that the path bends round.) Anyhow, that night I offered this boy what I reckoned he needed to hold him. I looked on it as giving. But it wasn't like no kind of giving *I* ever saw. I just laid back still in the dark—I couldn't see him—and he did what he had to do, and I was the one got caught with what *he* gave. His burden is swelling up in me right this minute without no name but Mustian. Oh, I *held* the boy. But I don't want him now. All this time I have lived on the hope he would change some day before it was too late and come home and calm down and learn how to talk to me and maybe even listen, and we would have a long life together—him and me—and be happy sometimes and get us children that would look like him and have his name and answer when we called. I just hoped that. But he hasn't changed. He said he would ride me to Dillon tonight and take me to Norfolk after Christmas to spend my life shut up in a

rented room while he sells motorcycles to fools—me
waiting out my baby sick as a dog, eating Post Toasties
and strong pork liver which would be all he could af-
ford and pressing his shirts and staring out a window in
my spare time at concrete roads and folks that look like
they hate each other. He offered me that. But that isn't
changing—not the way I hoped—so what I have done,
I will sit home and pay for. I am not glad, you understand, but I ain't asking him to share what trouble I
brought on myself.' "

Then Mr. Isaac moved and Rosacoke saw him
again. His head turned from her and bowed and his
lips parted, whispering to the dark where Sammy was,
and since it fulfilled her thought, she halfway expected
his hand to point her way, but Sammy's hand stretched
out—just his hand—and covered Mr. Isaac's for a second. Then the live fingers flicked to his mouth, and he
faced her again and ground his jaws one time, looking
almost satisfied. He was cracking candy under the music, and when he had swallowed, Sammy leaned forward out of the dark to wipe his chin with a handkerchief. Rosacoke saw first thing that Sammy was
wearing the blue wool suit he had worn to Mildred's
funeral, and with his face held there before her, she
strained to draw out some sign that would prove his
part in Mildred's baby, but he finished his wiping too
soon and gave a quick look towards her and smiled
with his eyes to show he knew before leaning back.

And Rosacoke knew she could not speak a word of
what she had thought, not to Mr. Isaac. Saying it to
him would mean telling Sammy—Sammy in the dark
with all he knew—and anyhow what good was that
news to him?—age eighty-two, claiming he couldn't die
but dead already in half his body, the other half

shielded as always, hoping to live on to ninety and equal his father, and not understanding, after all this time not knowing half *she* knew. So she thought, "He don't even know me. He has not known me all these years—not my name. He can't know me now in this costume, and I reckon he is far better off."

The Shepherds were coming to the middle of their song. Nearer the goal, their hands gripped tighter on the basket, and their voices washed strong over Frederick to Rosacoke and brought her back—

> *The cattle are lowing,*
> *The poor baby wakes,*
> *But little Lord Jesus*
> *No crying He makes.*

She had not thought of Frederick since the Shepherds began, and a chill of fright twitched at the roots of her hair. She said to herself, "I have not done my duty," and slowly, testing, her eyes worked down. But Macey behind her had shifted, and his great shadow hid the baby. She reckoned he was safe though, and she looked out straight before her over the Shepherds to the back of the church. Mama was supposed to be there, waiting to turn on lights at the end, but the back was dark as the night outside, and she narrowed her eyes to find her. What she found was four black figures against the wall—one that was Mama and three together in robes that were Milo and Rato and Wesley Beavers. When the Shepherds finished, the Wise Men would come.

And the Shepherds were curving onwards—

> *Be near us, Lord Jesus,*
> *We ask Thee to stay*
> *Close by us forever*
> *And love us, we pray—*

so for somewhere to look, hoping to rest her mind on
something calm, Rosacoke bent forward over the basket. She could not see till her face was nearly at the
rim. But Frederick had been seeing her. With the Shepherds singing at his left and his Daddy standing over
him and his three blood sisters giving off the light, still
he had set his eyes on her. She couldn't know why or
for how long, but she was glad a little, and at first he
seemed peaceful as if he knew who he saw, as if in all
his secret thoughts there was anyhow no fear—serious
but peaceful, wrapped loose in a Gupton-blue blanket
with bare arms free and only his fingers moving as if a
slow breeze lifted them one by one. He didn't seem
cold but Rosacoke thought she could cover him better,
and she put out a hand. He watched it come and when
it touched, his eyes coiled against her and his fingers
clamped and his lips spread to a slow black hole. Rosacoke drew back her hand and her face and thought in
a rush, "Now I must wait while he makes up his mind
to cry or be calm." The Shepherds saw him too, threat-
ening to break up their song, and they lowered their
voices in hope—

> *Bless all the dear children*
> *In Thy tender care*—

but Frederick gave no hope of blessing. He hung fire
before their eyes, every muscle in his body cocked
against Rosacoke but *waiting* as if he would give her
this last chance to offer what he needed before he
called on the church at large. She could see that but
she couldn't move. She didn't know a thing to offer,
and she said to herself, "I certainly don't have much
luck with babies." Then she looked up again—to the
dim front pew where she reckoned Marise would be—

and her eyes asked desperate for help. Marise was there all right, settled around her hard new belly, tireder already than Mr. Isaac and staring at her family performing—the ones standing up, Macey and the girls. She couldn't see Frederick in his basket, but he had nursed her dry an hour before and swallowed ten drops of paregoric so her mind was at ease about him, and she didn't even notice Rosacoke.

The Shepherds crept on to the end—

> *And take us to heaven*
> *To dwell with Thee there.*

Then they lifted their hands off the manger that rocked again and they stood, and Frederick turned to them, suddenly seeming calmer. But the Shepherds were finished. They were leaving. They ducked their heads to Frederick as a bow and filed to the rear of the choir and picked up candles from a chair and took fire from the Angels, adding that much to the light. When they were gone Frederick lay on through the quiet, still turned to the side, and he lay through the preacher's voice, "Now when Jesus was born in Bethlehem of Judaea in the days of Herod the King, behold, there came Wise Men from the east to Jerusalem, saying, 'Where is he that is born King of the Jews? for we have seen his star in the east and are come to worship him' . . . and lo, the star which they saw in the east went before them till it came and stood over where the young child was," and when the Wise Men began their song, the distant voices seemed to calm him more than anything had—

> *We three kings of Orient are*
> *Bearing gifts we traverse afar . . .*

His fingers went loose again and his stiff legs bent a little, but he didn't look back to Rosacoke, and that was for the best because at those first words, the cords of her chest took hold of her heart and a frown spread from her eyes. She was seeing the far dark wall. They were still at the back in darkness—the three men. They would sing one verse together. Then they would light their candles and come forward separate, offering separate verses. But before they moved, dim as they were, the sight of them deepened Rosacoke's frown, and when Mama struck a match and held it to a candle, then Rosacoke was worse. But that first candle was Rato's—it lit only *his* face—and as he began his verse and his march, she felt a little ease. He couldn't sing—nobody expected him to—but he knew his words, and he moaned them in time to his long, shaking steps, looking down as he came.

> *Born a babe on Bethlehem's plain,*
> *Gold I bring to crown Him again—*
> *King forever, ceasing never*
> *Over us all to reign.*

That much brought him almost to the choir, and the dark two at the back sent him on as they joined in the chorus—

> *O star of wonder, star of night,*
> *Star with royal beauty bright,*
> *Westward leading, still proceeding,*
> *Guide us to the perfect light.*

He came till his toes knocked hard on the first step of the choir, and looking only down, he bowed low enough to set a brass bowl on the floor by the basket. It represented gold, his gift. Then he unbent upwards

and stepped to one side and rocked his face onto Rosacoke. She met his great yellow eyes and thought it was
the first time in clear memory he had *faced* her so she
smoothed her frown the best she could and tried to
match his simple unrecognizing graveness. Then she
waited while he searched her face, wondering, "Why is
he staring at me like this? Have I changed that much
since supper?" And feeling as she did—so low—she
reckoned that was right. Maybe nobody knew her at
all. Maybe nobody in all those dark pews saw what she
thought they were seeing. Maybe what they saw was
changed too far to know—not by a blue cambric costume but by what she had done that night seven weeks
ago, by what she was *making* that grew in her body this
instant not ten inches from her heart, twisted on itself
in the dark, using her blood for its own. Maybe that
face was showing through hers for all to see—shapeless,
blind, nameless face. Needing some kind of answer
she looked to Mr. Isaac. But if he knew her the secret
would die with him. *Sammy* knew. Sammy saw both
faces, surely—her old first face and this new one, working under it—but Sammy was out of sight. And Guptons, Aycocks, Smileys, Riggans, Overbys, Mama and
Milo and Wesley himself, and Frederick if he would
turn back and face her—what were they all seeing, what
did they *know* from the way she looked? And supposing she stood up now right under that star and testified,
"I am Rosacoke Mustian and the reason I look so
changed tonight is because I am working on a baby
that I made by mistake and am feeding right now with
my blood against my better wishes—but a baby I am
meaning to *have* and give my Daddy's name to if it
lives and is a boy, one I will try to raise happy, and I'd
thank you for helping me any way you can"—what

would they say to that? They would not believe her at
first, and in time, when they did, they would turn
their heads and never speak a word, much less offer
help, and Mama's heart would break. She looked up at
Rato again. His eyes were still on her so—silent, with
her lips—she said "Hello, Rato" and tried to smile, but
the smile didn't come and Rato didn't answer, just
looked down again as if what he had seen would last
him a long time yet.

The only thing like an answer came from the
back. Mama struck another match and lit up Milo and
he started forwards. *He* was singing though he didn't
know the meaning of half he sang, didn't care—

> *Frankincense to offer have I.*
> *Incense owns a Deity nigh—*

and he walked so fast he reached the choir with two
lines to sing—

> *Prayer and praising all men raising,*
> *Worship Him, God on high.*

Then all three began the chorus, and Milo bowed to
give his gift. What he laid by the basket was nothing to
him but a cheap jewel box he had won on a gas-station
punchboard six years before (he had never smelled
incense in his life), and Macey, that he looked at first
when he rose, was nothing but Macey-dressed-funny
and the same for Rato and Shepherds and Angels and
his sister Rosa and, at first, even Frederick. As he
grinned at them all (he crossed his eyes at Baby Sister),
they could see he was making up jokes to tell when the
show was over—all except Rosacoke. She didn't see
him, not at first, not his face. She had not really faced
Milo since the nineteenth of November, the morning

she promised to stick with him, when they struck out for Raleigh and she got Wesley's letter and read it and when she understood—stopped by that dead field and that pecan tree—went back on her word and told Milo to take her home, leaving him his whole burden. So she looked down at Frederick when the chorus began, but Frederick was studying Milo or maybe the fire in his hand, and as he looked Milo must have made some crazy face—Frederick oared with both legs and though he didn't smile, he held up a hand. Rosacoke could see—anybody could have seen—that the hand was for Milo, and still singing, Milo put out his free hand, and Frederick took one dark finger and closed on it and drew it towards his mouth. Rosacoke had to look up then, and what she saw was almost that first Milo, the one who could tear her heart, and the look that grew on him was awful to her—not a frown but the way he had looked that night in Mary's kitchen—and she had to change it. She had to draw Frederick's attention to herself. She reached in the basket and commenced arranging the blanket, and Frederick turned her way as she hoped, letting go of Milo's finger. That was all she intended but Frederick meant more, and when she took back her hands, he whimpered once—not loud—and huddled in readiness. Rosacoke didn't move. She braced herself for what would come next, but behind her Macey had seen everything. He bent to her ear— "Rosa, pick him up. He's fixing to yell." She heard him (everybody heard him for yards and stiffened) but she didn't move. She shook her head and said just with her lips, "Frederick, *I* ain't what you need"—and to herself, recalling the last time she said such a thing, "I guess I can't run this time." The chorus stopped. Milo stepped aside and Rosacoke looked to the back.

And she couldn't—couldn't run. Mama struck the last match and held it out. The candle caught fire and Wesley Beavers had a sudden face that he was bringing on, a black bandanna hiding his hair, a black robe crossed at his neck—

> *Myrrh is mine, its bitter perfume*
> *Breathes a life of gathering gloom.*

The frown cut deeper into her eyes, and Frederick whimpered stronger than before. She thought, "Take a-hold, Rosacoke. You are *free*," and she tried to turn to Frederick, but Wesley, coming slow, was six steps away, and what she saw held her locked—just his face borne forward on a candle through eighty people towards her, swarmed with warning of the ruins and lives he would make—

> *Sorrowing, sighing, bleeding, dying,*
> *Sealed in the stone-cold tomb.*

Her head rolled back and her lips fell open as if she would greet some killing bird, but anybody watching— her Mama and Milo, even Marise Gupton, even Rato —saw her suck one breath in pain.

Then Wesley was at the basket, looking down, his verse finished. He stooped to place his gift (a covered butter dish) and stood for the chorus, and as it began he looked over Frederick to Rosacoke—offering his face, his real gift, the only gift he always gave, without even knowing, but it pressed against her now through six feet of air like a knife held waiting on her skin—his eyes which had seen her that awful way in the broom-straw field (her secret and then her hate), which had seen other women (God knew how many) laid back like her but giving him things she could not even guess, and under the bandanna his ears that had heard those women say "Yes," and then his mouth that had never moved once to make the word "love," not to her any- how. He was not frowning but he was not glad—she could see that plain—just waiting. He had trapped him- self and then done what he saw as his duty—*offered* his duty—and now he waited for her. Before she could shake her head and set him free, a voice cut up through the chorus. It was Frederick at last and Macey who could only see Rosacoke's shivering back, bent to whis- per, "Hand him here. I'm his Daddy, Rosa."

She was at her worst. She knew it. And she found the strength to try that—to try handing Frederick on— not because it would save the show but to save herself from running or screaming. Somehow she got both hands in the basket and under Frederick, and she leaned to take his weight. The minute he was in the air, his crying stopped. Rosacoke knew she could not lay him back, not yet, and she knew how strange it would look if she gave him to Macey now so she brought him on to the groove of her lap. He was too long to lie there straight, but his legs jackknifed till he fit, and his head weighed back in her hands. He probed once easy with his feet at her belly, but he seemed con- tent and Rosacoke said to herself, "Look at Frederick. Think about Frederick." And she thought, slow, to fill time, "You are named Frederick Gupton. You are Ma- rise Gupton's fourth baby, and I think you are eight months old which means you were born last April. You are long for your age, seems like, but most of your length is in your neck. You sure got the Gupton neck—long as most folks' leg—and your *eyes* are your Daddy's and your flapping ears. But you got Marise's black hair, poor thing—straight as walking canes. You look about as much like Baby Jesus as Rato does."

But he wasn't studying her. He was using her hands as something to roll his head on, limber as an owl, and take his bearings, and Rosacoke let him look but she didn't follow his eyes. It was hard enough, watching him switch that face onto various ones, quick as a whip and solemn, and waiting till it came her turn. For some time though he stayed on the Wise Men. They were singing their last to the star—

> *Westward leading, still proceeding,*
> *Guide us to the perfect light—*

and when they were done, Baby Sister and her Angels stepped closer forward and began "Silent Night," very loud. But they didn't interest Frederick and after they sang two lines, he looked to Rosacoke and put up his arms to her and strained his head off her knees till he flushed bright red. At first she thought, "Frederick, I ain't who you think I am" (meaning she was not Marise). But his hands stayed up, twitching, and his head still strained so Rosacoke bent down and touched her cheek to his—his was warmer—and when she rose she could smell something strange. Trying to name it she only saw Landon Allgood in her mind, laid out at Mount Moriah in late July or digging a grave five weeks ago or just now heading for Mary's to eat, with half Mama's holly as payment, and Christmas coming which would be the anniversary of his toes. She bent again, not as far. Then she knew what it was— Frederick was the source. He was fragrant with pare-goric—his breath—and by all rights he never should have waked (even now his eyes were tired). But his

hands were reaching. He meant her to take him up—
there was no doubting that and Rosacoke recalled Mary
saying how Sledge was a *shoulder* baby so she gave in
to Frederick and lifted him to her shoulder, thinking,
"He can face his Daddy now and feel at home and
sleep, I hope." But he didn't stay there ten seconds.
The Angels still didn't hold him, not even their lights,
and his head rolled down to her chest, heavy on his
neck as five pounds of seed. She thought, "Thank the
Lord. He is sleepy" and raised his head with her hand.
He was not too sleepy to show he didn't want that. His
head came down again—wandered slower this time—
so Rosacoke left him to take his will, and looking over
people to the back where her Mama was dark, she
canceled her sight and fixed her mind on Frederick's
weight (that grew every second) and his heat that crept
through blanket and costume into her cold side, and
soon she was far from him and then farther—from herself and Delight Baptist Church and everybody in it,
her mind roaming empty and freer than it had been
since the first time she saw the deer in broad daylight at
the edge of the broomstraw ring, half hid in trees but
watching, waiting (till Mildred said "Great God
A-mighty"), then going, loud in the leaves.

It didn't last much longer than the deer—her
blank roaming. The Angels paused at the end of their
first verse, and as they took breath the new sound Frederick made brought her back. He had worked his head
to her chest, and he was chewing the cloth just over her
heart—not wild or fast or sharp (he had three teeth)
but wet and steady as if he had all night, had years of
time and the trust of food someday and could gnaw
his way through granite rock, not to speak of cambric
and her white skin, to get what he reckoned was his.

Her chest shrank inwards from his mouth. She pushed his head away as if his spit could scald, and she thought, "I am not who he *thinks* I am." But before she could shift him to a safe position, she had to look up and half-way play her part in the show. The Angels had come to—

> *Darkness flies, all is light.*
> *Shepherds hear the Angels sing—*

and that was a sign for the Shepherds to move. They stepped from behind the Angels and Macey and down the two choir steps, and they knelt again at the basket, not touching it this time. They were the reason Rosacoke looked up. It was her part to nod at them and try to smile. She did nod, accepting their praise for the baby, and she tried to smile to show she knew each one—Moulton Ayscue, John Arthur Bobbitt, Bracey Overby—had known them all their lives, but they didn't return her acquaintance, didn't smile, only bobbed their chins and turned to Frederick, where he was.

He was back at her chest, one hand pressing hard enough to flush out his blood and his open mouth laid on the peak of her breast. But his jaws were moving slower and his eyes were shut. Rosacoke saw him, where he wanted to be, and waited a little and then gave in —"If that's all it takes to help you rest, go ahead."

He went ahead, lowering himself deeper into sleep with every pull of his jaws—every pull weaker than the last—his breaths coming farther and farther apart, strained like sighs through his nose, and his eyelids heavy enough to stay down for hours. Rosacoke wondered was he dreaming yet—at first his shut face offered no sign. She asked herself, "Reckon what does he

dream when he dreams?" and while the Angels finished
a verse, she studied him and tried to guess. "Maybe he
dreams about getting born last April in Marise and
Macey's iron bed, coming out easy as an Indian baby
but howling till they got him washed and turned him
loose on Marise's breast. Or maybe he can see further
back than April"—she counted back in her mind—
"maybe he recalls being made one evening in late July
when it had been hot all day and the night was no
help, and Macey was twisting in the bed, wringing wet,
and then there come up a cooling storm, and when it
passed and the rain frogs commenced outside, he felt
relief and touched Marise and came down on her in
the dark, and she took what he gave for her fourth
burden, without even seeing him."

When she finished that, Frederick's jaws had
stopped, and his fingers had eased against her. She
lowered the hand that held his Gupton neck—to cradle
him better. His head settled in her arms as if she was
his natural rest, and his whole face rolled towards her.
Rolling, he flared out his ears even further and pressed
out his hair stiff on her sleeve, and she thought again,
"If Baby Jesus looked like you—poor Mary," but then
she noticed his life, where it beat hid and awful in each
bare temple and—visible, blue—in the hot veins of his
eyelids and his standing ears, filling him sure as an unlabeled seed with all he would be, the ruins he would
make and the lives. "Wonder could he dream about
that?" she thought, "—about growing up and someday
(standing in a field or up a pecan tree) seeing a girl
that he felt for and testing till he knew it was love and
speaking his offer and taking her home and then one
evening, making on her some child that would have
his name and signs of him and the girl all in its face—

maybe even signs of Marise and Macey? Wonder could he be dreaming that right now?"

But he offered no answer and the Angels came to—

See the eastern Wise Men bring
Gifts and homage to our King—

and the Wise Men stepped back to kneel with the Shepherds. Rosacoke's part was to look up and nod to them but she couldn't. She looked on at Frederick and went on guessing, to calm herself—"Wonder is he dreaming about *me*, and does he know who I am?" But that was no calming thought, no help. "He don't know me from Adam. Of course he don't. He has not laid eyes on me since late July at Mason's Lake when I was not myself, grieving for Mildred. If he has thought about me for three seconds even, he thinks I am just Marise that can drop my babies like a mangy hound and flip out my bosoms in public to stop them yelling." She looked up to her right, needing somebody to *know* her and nod their acquaintance, but all she met was Mr. Isaac awake in his chair, still not understanding, and Sammy dark beside him and at the back her Mama dark as the night outside, and in the front pew Marise staring tired across her to Macey, and Rato and Milo her own blood brothers, five feet away, not facing her— not one soul to own they knew her.

She looked to Wesley. There was nowhere else to look. He was kneeling tall back of John Arthur Bobbitt with his face and his eyes on her, having offered his duty and with nothing to do but wait for her answer so he could plan his life, still not frowning but not glad, smiling no more than her father when he was a boy before he changed, in a tan photograph on a pier by the ocean with another boy blurred beside him. She stayed facing him. He held her like a chain. Then she drew one breath, hard, and said what she suddenly knew—to herself—what he had showed her, "Wesley knows me. After all Wesley knows me." And she knew that was her answer, for all it meant, the answer she would have to give when the pageant was over and Wesley drove her home and stopped in the yard and made his offer again—"Are we riding to Dillon tonight?"—because it was her duty, for all it would mean.

But also it was her wish. She saw that too. She faced that now and she spoke it as a trial to her mind— her answer. But once she had said it, even silent, it boiled up in her like cold spring water through leaves, rising low from her belly till it filled her chest and throat and spilled up into her mouth and beat against her teeth. She had to speak it or drown, and who could she speak to but Frederick Gupton in her arms asleep? She bent again and touched his ear with her lips and said it to him, barely whispered it—"Yes"—and wished him, silent, a long happy life. When she rose his face was still towards her, breathing out Landon every breath. He seemed the safest thing still, seemed shut for the night, so while they sang the last verse around her (Baby Sister climbing through the rest pure as day), she looked on at him, and under her eyes his lips commenced to move, just the corners at first, slow as if they were pulled like tides by the moon, as if he might wake to end some dream, but his eyes didn't open, didn't flicker, and his lips pulled on till at last he had made what was almost a smile, for his own reasons and for no more than three seconds but as if, even in his sleep, he knew of love.

REYNOLDS PRICE

Born in Macon, North Carolina in 1933, Reynolds
Price attended North Carolina schools and received
his Bachelor of Arts degree from Duke University.
As a Rhodes Scholar he studied for three years at
Merton College, Oxford, receiving the Bachelor of
Letters with a thesis on Milton. In 1958 he re-
turned to Duke where he is now James B. Duke
Professor of English. His first novel *A Long and
Happy Life* appeared in 1962. A volume of stories
The Names and Faces of Heroes appeared in 1963.
In the years since, he has published *A Generous
Man* (a novel), *Love and Work* (a novel), *Perma-
nent Errors* (stories), *Things Themselves* (essays
and scenes), *The Surface of Earth* (a novel), *Early
Dark* (a play), *A Palpable God* (translations from
the Bible with an essay on the origins and life
of narrative), *The Source of Light* (a novel), *Vital Provisions* (poems), *Private Contentment* (a
play), *Kate Vaiden* (a novel) and *The Laws of
Ice* (poems). His first two novels and the story "A
Chain of Love" are now collected in a single volume *Mustian*. His books have been translated into
fifteen languages.